"Hard boiled pulp, hot off the press. The writing team of JB Kohl and Eric Beetner give the middle finger to polite crime writing and splatter the pages of *Over Their Heads* with foul mouthed, two-fisted action delivered in a hail of bullets. Neo-noir, transgressive fans will cheer. Drawing room mystery readers may need smelling salts. Don't say you weren't warned."

—Anonymous-9, author of
Hard Bite and *Bite Harder*

"*Over Their Heads* is a stripped down hot-rod of a novel. JB Kohl and Eric Beetner keep things fast and tight, with a gasp or a laugh on pretty much every page as an assortment of would-be badasses try to track down some missing drugs. It's a comedy of errors, scored with the sound of gunfire."

—Jake Hinkson, author
of *The Big Ugly*

"*Over Their Heads* is a real tour-de-force from the writers that brought you *One too Many Blows to the Head*. A full-blown crime noir that will keep you on the edge of your seat!"

—Bill Craig, author of the
Marlow Key West Mysteries
and the Decker P.I. mysteries

Praise for the work of
JB Kohl and Eric Beetner

One Too Many Blows To The Head

"*One Too Many Blows to the Head* feels like a long-lost pulp you find in a favorite bookstore. A delicious mix of classic hardboiled grit and the heart-heavy world of film noir, it's a one-sitting read that sends you back to a lost time of fight halls, Chicago boys and last chances."

—Megan Abbott, author of *Dare Me* and *Queenpin*

"A powerful tale of vengeance, rife with pounding action and colorful, complex characters. *One Too Many Blows To The Head* is a first round knock-out!"
—Stephen Jay Schwartz, *LA Times* best-selling author of *Boulevard and Beat*

"The prose is hardboiled and lean, and there's plenty of violence. There's a surprise or two along the way, and you'll want to know what happens to Fokoli and Ray. They're deeply flawed, but Beetner and Kohl keep them human, which is quite an accomplishment when you consider the circumstances."
—Bill Crider, author of the Sheriff Dan Rhodes series

Borrowed Trouble

"Meticulous historical detail slams you into the hard boiled world of Ray Ward and Dean Fokoli as they use hard fists and cold steel to knock the shiny off Hollywood's glitter. *Borrowed Trouble* is like a talented fighter—powerful, quick, and hard to put down."
—Rebecca Cantrell, NYT best-selling author of the Hannah Vogel mysteries

"For a knockout punch of hardboiled, look no further than *Borrowed Trouble*, sequel to the period noir *One Too Many Blows To The Head*. You'll want to go the distance with Ray Ward, a tough-luck protagonist who knows how to hit where it counts!"
—Kelli Stanley, author of *City of Dragons* and *City of Secrets*

"Everyone has a short list of books that stayed with them long after they turned the last page—add *Borrowed Trouble* to mine. Eric Beetner and J.B. Kohl have vividly re-created 1941 Los Angeles, ripping apart the city's glamorous façade to reveal the cold noir heart beneath. With sharp writing, head-spinning twists, and pair of protagonists haunted by memory and loss, this is pulp fiction at its finest."
—Hilary Davidson, author of *The Damage Done* and *Blood Always Tells*

OVER THEIR HEADS

ALSO BY JB KOHL & ERIC BEETNER

One Too Many Blows to the Head
Borrowed Trouble

ALSO BY JB KOHL

The Deputy's Widow

ALSO BY ERIC BEETNER

The Devil Doesn't Want Me
Rumrunners
The Year I Died Seven Times
The Backlist (with Frank Zafiro)
Criminal Economics
Dig Two Graves
White Hot Pistol
Stripper Pole at the End of the World
A Bouquet of Bullets (stories)
Fightcard: Split Decision
Fightcard: A Mouth Full of Blood

JB KOHL & ERIC BEETNER

OVER THEIR HEADS

Copyright 2015 by JB Kohl & Eric Beetner
First Print Edition: June 2015

All rights reserved. No part of the book may be reproduced in any form or by any electronic or mechanical means, including information storage and retrieval systems, without permission in writing from the publisher, except by a reviewer who may quote brief passages in a review.

Down & Out Books
3959 Van Dyke Rd, Ste. 265
Lutz, FL 33558
www.DownAndOutBooks.com

The characters and events in this book are fictitious. Any similarity to real persons, living or dead, is coincidental and not intended by the author.

Cover design by JT Lindroos

ISBN: 1937495949
ISBN-13: 978-1-937495-94-7

1
CLYDE

If Madeline didn't go into labor we'd be eating steak tonight. In a restaurant. Because I would have enough cash to take her out for a change. I'd have money for dinner and clothes and a vacation and enough left over for the baby's college and graduate school—anything else our kid could want.

I rummaged through my sock drawer for a pair that matched. A wife at nine-and-a-half-months pregnant didn't feel the best. In the past Madeline had been meticulous about organizing my sock drawer, folding and pairing them in neat rows. Those days were gone now, along with the days of creased khakis and starched shirts. My kind and beautiful wife had changed to someone pasty, swollen, and, yeah I'm gonna say it...bitchy.

For now, at least, she was asleep, hand resting over her protruding belly, mouth slightly open. In these moments, before she woke up and started to cry over her swollen ankles and nag me about the long hours I spent at the rental lot, before she opened her mouth and swore at me and the dick that happens to reside between my legs, which was clearly responsible for getting her in this predicament in the first place, marriage vows or no...in these moments when it was just me digging in my sock drawer for a mate to the only one I could find, when I picked up my khakis from the floor and shook out yesterday's wrinkles...I would watch her sleep and she was just my wife, the woman I fell in love with.

I saw this movie once. It was one of those chick flicks I took her to on our last anniversary. Normally I don't go in for that sort of thing, but it was our anniversary and that's a time she tends to get sentimental and I'm almost always guaranteed sex. So I figure on those nights the least I can do is take her to a movie she wants to see, even if I have zero interest in it. I don't even remember what the movie was about. Well, it was about a couple, that's for sure, but the thing I remember is that the woman was pregnant. I mean hugely pregnant. And in one scene, the guy in that film bends over his just-about-to-pop pregnant wife and kisses her stomach. When that happened on the screen, next to me, in the theater, Madeline sighed and put her hand over her heart, and her breath hitched just the tiniest bit like it does when she is just about to cry or like when she watches those dog food commercials. That scene really got to her. I always remembered that moment, the moment in that movie when Madeline was moved by something so simple. We didn't know it at the time, but she was already seven weeks pregnant and when we found out a week later and realized it was really, really real, I remembered that scene and played it out a hundred times in my head. I knew there would come a time when I'd lean over her and kiss her belly because it would make her happy. And, I don't know, I guess I imagined myself whispering something profound and kind to her. So I had been biding my time, waiting until she was tired and heavy and hating being pregnant, because all the books told me that was exactly how it was going to be. I wanted it to be perfect. I guess the time never seemed perfect.

Because today I watched her with my socks in my hand, and just felt...tired. So I turned and walked out. I tiptoed so she wouldn't wake up and I shut the door behind me as quietly as I could. Hollywood and that damn movie could kiss my ass. And so could the goddamn actress with the rail thin legs and a belly with no stretch marks. Madeline was a real woman. Despite it all, despite being Misery's Deity at the moment, she was a real woman, the mother of my child. She was mine. And while this filled me with pride and gratitude, mostly these days I was filled with fear.

I toed through the pile of shoes at the front door, settling on a pair of bland loafers, and mentally ran over the day's plans in my head.

ONE: Get to work, open the rental lot. If I was honest, this was my favorite part of every day. I liked the lot. It was mine. I had named it after myself, hadn't I? Clyde McDowd Rentals was, in a way, my first kid. And now, after marriage and with a real, actual kid on the way, it was the one thing that was entirely mine. It was clean, organized, filled with files and the smell of the pink cleaning solution the janitor used late at night. It was white tile floor and fluorescent lights. It was the roar of airplanes taking off and landing at Richmond International. It was business men and families. And somewhere along the way, it started to bring in a lot more money than it should have. Which is why I really, really needed to be at work on time today.

I looked down at the scuffed loafer I had pulled from the pile of shoes. How could one couple own so many shoes? Even my shoes were something Madeline picked out for me. The house. The carpet. The paint. The towels in the bathroom. But Clyde McDowd Rentals? Not so, baby. Not so. I drifted into the kitchen and sank into one of the rickety wooden chairs at our vintage table and pulled on a sock.

TWO: Check to make sure the Chevy Tahoe was ready to go. The ceiling seams needed to be perfect, the packets had to be laying right, behind a soft, thin layer of sponge. I always put a pack of Winstons in the glove compartment for the driver. Never hurts to kiss a little ass, just in case. I froze with the sock halfway on. Shit. I forgot the Winstons.

THREE: Stop and pick up Winstons.

The mattress in the bedroom groaned as Madeline pushed herself up. The giantess hath awakened, I thought, not unkindly. Hell, if Madeline had been her normal, petite, good-humored self, she would have laughed too. And some day, I was sure I'd tell her my vision of her at nine months pregnant—an angry, towering woman crushing all in her path, and she would laugh and punch me in the arm and say she loved me.

I'd tell her about all of this one day and not just how grouchy she was. I'd tell her about everything I'd done for her, about everything I sacrificed, the risks I took, the plans I made for us, for our family.

Today was not going to be that day.

Today I shoved my feet in my shoes and popped a piece of bread in the toaster. I heard her approach from the other room and pasted a smile on my face. She opened the door and shuffled into the kitchen, her legs swollen, beautiful dark hair cascading down her back. My smile became a real one. No matter what, it was easy to love Madeline. All of it for you, I thought. "Want coffee?" I asked.

She didn't answer but reached to the cupboard above the coffee pot, stomach resting on the counter, hands fumbling for filters and coffee beans. "Let me do that," I said. "You sit down. Put your feet up."

"It won't help," she said. "Nothing does. I'm a house." She turned to look at me and I caught a glimpse of the clock on the stove at the same time I caught the look on her face. 7:45 on the clock. Worry on her face. Car lot opened at 8:00. I had been told to expect the driver any time after 8:10.

Christ on a cracker.

"You're not a house," I said, moving to hug her. She allowed the touch and rested her head on my shoulder. Her hair smelled like that really good shampoo she uses. 7:46.

FOUR: Move Chevy Tahoe to the back part of the lot under the maple that tended to shit sap on cars all day long. No one ever wanted to drive a sap-speckled car. It was another reason I put the Winstons in the glove box.

Madeline lifted her head from my shoulder and tried to smile. Then she burst into tears. I walked her to the table and sat her down. 7:47.

"I don't know," she said, her face in her hands. "I just don't know. I feel like this is it. Like this kid is coming out of me today. I'm so tired." She slumped forward and rested her head on her forearms. "I am not up to this today. My back hurts. And why didn't we find out the sex?"

Because you didn't want to. You said it was a good thing to be surprised. You said we wanted to experience the wonder of birth like they did in the old days. "We just didn't," I said. I ran a hand over her hair and kissed the top of her head. Then I pulled the filters from the cupboard, poured water in the coffee pot, and spilled coffee beans on the floor. 7:50.

Madeline looked at the beans. "I can't clean that up. I can't bend down and clean that up." She sniffled and started crying again.

"You don't have to, babe. I've got it."

"Those are expensive beans, too."

FIVE: Close shop doors at 5:00 p.m. and wait for

instructions. At some point this evening, I would receive directions to the envelope containing a debit card and access to an account with my money. It was safer than cash and smarter, and I had done it a few times before already. This time was big, though. This was the last one, the one that would set us up forever.

I swept up the beans and tossed them in the trash. 7:52. I was late. There was no way I'd make it there in time.

I buttered the toast and spread peanut butter on it. Then I set it in front of Madeline and kissed her on the forehead. "I've got to make a call. I'll be right back."

I knew I should offer to stay with her, to sit and hold her hand and stroke her hair and reassure her. If she only knew that this was all for her. I stepped out onto the front stoop and auto dialed Brent's cell.

There was fumbling as he picked up and a frazzled, "Yeah."

"You at the office?"

I heard him clear his throat. "In the car in the Starbuck's drive-through. Want anything?"

"Need you to open."

"Sure."

"No. Listen. I need to you to open. This is important."

I listened as Brent ordered a Venti Caramel Macchiato and then came back on the line. "You sure you don't want something?"

"Nothing."

"Right. Open the lot. Got it."

"Shut the fuck up and listen to me, Brent. There's a Chevy Tahoe near the front. I need you to jockey it to the back under the maple tree. Got it?"

"Chevy. Maple. Tahoe. That's a shitty tree. What do you got against that car?"

I pinched the bridge of my nose. "Just do it. Don't fuck up. I'll be there as soon as I can."

I could almost hear Brent shrug through the phone. I had no idea what was worse. Having Madeline pissed at me or trusting the car arrangements to Brent. It's like asking how do you want to die? Fire or drawn and quartered?

2
BRENT

What the hell was up his ass? Clyde used to be such a great boss. I guessed it was the kid that had him on edge recently. I mean, I took the job because the hours were good, the pressure was low and the policy on smoking was lax.

I watched all those Hertz and Enterprise jerks running around in their matching shirts and scripted sales pitches and I thanked sweet Jesus that wasn't me. Still never thought I'd be renting cars out at the airport. Beats digging ditches, as my dad always said.

I tried to understand what Clyde was going through though. A baby. That's heavy. And him being a business owner. Entrepreneur. Sole breadwinner. I know I'm not ready for that yet.

I kept feeling like something had been up for a while now, but I couldn't put my finger on it. He would get all sweaty about once a month, giving orders on certain cars like this Tahoe now. When he told me his wife was pregnant I put two and two together. Lately, seemed like they added up to five.

Not my business, though. We were friends, sure, but his life was his and my life was mine. To each his own, as my mom used to say. They said a lot of stuff, my parents.

I opened the rental counter only five minutes late. Not bad for me. I'd almost finished refilling the brochure holders and the maps to Colonial Williamsburg, when the first customers of the day came in.

A family on vacation, cranky from the flight which must have left wherever they came from while it was still dark outside. I'd be cranky, too. A mom with short, sensible hair and twenty extra pounds around the middle. A dad with a bald top and a ring of sad looking wisps circling the rim of his skull. He toted about eighty extra pounds around his belt line. Eight a.m. and already sweating like a hog.

They pulled enough bags for a two-week trip and two kids who looked like puberty had run them down in the street driving a Sherman tank. A boy and a girl. They looked to be in the midst of a contest for which one could grow the most pimples. A dead tie so far, from what I could see.

"Morning. How can I help you?" I said. First one of the day gets my special "helpful guy" treatment.

Dad stepped in front of his depressing family and took charge. One look at him and I could tell the only time in his life he got to take charge of anything was with a pudgy, given-up wife and two kids destined to live out the rest of their lives waiting for their awkward phase to end. Congrats, Pops, you're king of the royal family of kill-me-if-it-ever-happens-to-me.

"We have a reservation. Griffin."

All business, this guy. Better than the chit chat of some jerk who got off an eight-hour flight and needed to vent about the shitty flight attendants and sub-standard food.

"Okay," I said. "Let me pull up your reservation."

I typed his name into the computer and his page came on screen. Another good thing about being with a small, independent rental company is we can pretty much count all the rentals on two hands in a day. There's never a lot of searching for lost files around here.

"Here we go. Minivan, right?" As if I needed to look that up in the computer.

"Yes. Minivan. For two weeks." His wife fanned him with a folded up map. I hoped his face didn't turn any redder or I'd start to worry about the old guy having a heart attack in the lobby. The two sad sack kids stared blankly, the boy mouth-breathing through thick braces.

"That's mileage included," he sort of asked, sort of stated.

"Yes. Mileage included." I'm sure it made him feel like a real provider, a real hunter/gatherer to this family of Cro-Magnons.

"Dad, I'm hungry," the boy said.

"Yeah, me too," the girl followed up. Really? These lard-asses hungry? You don't say.

"We'll get breakfast as soon as we're out of here and on the road," he said in that typical annoyed dad way. I bet he couldn't wait to get behind the wheel so he could threaten them with the old, "If you don't knock it off I'll turn this car around and…" But if they were at an airport I doubted he was gonna drive them all the way home. Mileage or no mileage included.

"Where y'all from?" I asked while the rental form printed.

"Detroit," he said, clipped and sharp to let me know that was all the information I would be getting out of him.

I nodded. I figured I didn't need to tell him what a shithole he lived in, so I left it there.

"Here we are," I said. I read him all the particulars; he declined the insurance. They all do. Anyone renting from us was a cheap bastard, so they all turned down the insurance. I got his info and offered to do the walk through of the van with him.

"I think I know how a minivan works," he said.

"It's more just to check for any damage to the vehicle so you won't be liable upon return. And there may be a few things in the newer models you may not be familiar with."

"Da-a-a-ad," the boy said, his impatience showing like the big red zit on his nose.

"That's fine, just tell me what spot it's in and we'll get going. We still have a drive ahead of us to get to the beach."

"I don't know why you wouldn't let my dad pick us up," the wife said.

"I'm not gonna rely on your parents to get us around. What if we want to take a day trip?" He didn't hide his annoyance and I knew this was an argument that started back in Detroit.

"What day trips are we gonna take, Sean?"

"We at least want the freedom, Linda." He spat out her name with such a fermented venom. That one word, her name, had been marinated in all the years of marriage and all the variations on this argument they'd ever had, which I took to be many.

"You're in space twenty-three," I said, still in my early morning fake cheeriness. Besides, the Griffin family provided me with some great theater to start the day. The Fighting Griffins starring in Sad Suburban Vacation: A Tragedy.

"Thanks," he said and a bead of sweat broke loose from his empty forehead and ran down his nose to splash on my counter. If he saw it, he ignored it. The whole wheezing, squeaking mass of them turned as one and rolled out pushing, pulling and toting luggage almost as square as they were.

I sat back down, wiped the drop of sweat away with a napkin and lit my first smoke of the day, thankful my life wasn't as soul-crushing and shitty as that guy and his dumb-ass family. For me, right then behind the rental counter on a sunny Virginia day—payday no less—life was looking pretty good.

3
CLYDE

Despite being late, despite the forgotten cigarettes and the ten minute wait at the Gas 'N Gulp to pick them up, despite Madeline's tears, I smiled when I pulled into the lot. It was a scorcher of a day already. Jets were screaming a half mile away at the airport, and my lot was ready for renters.

The lot had it all: compacts, sub-compacts, convertibles, SUVs, luxury sedans, mid-size sedans and coupes, luxury coupes, mini vans, and full size vans. I had been considering adding RV rentals as well, but it was likely to be a couple of years before I was feeling ambitious enough for that. I needed to do more homework on the demand, and with the kid soon to be born, I wasn't eager to undertake any additional responsibility. Besides, I was spread a little too thin as it was.

I didn't look for the Tahoe under the maple. It was early and Brent would have parked it where I told him. He might be a grumbler, but he could be counted on to do what he was told. When I walked in, he stood at the twin filing cabinets in the front of the office, stuffing a rental agreement into a drawer.

"Remember your alphabet," I said. "A, B, C."

"Yeah. I got it." He gave a half smile. He acted pissed, but he was really shitty when it came to filing stuff. I kept him around because, in addition to doing what he was told, he didn't ask many questions and he didn't seem too interested in what I did when I wasn't standing right next to him. In fact, he seemed to try really hard to avoid me sometimes, which was just fine these days. The less we saw of one another, the better.

"Anyone come in?"

He gave me a gesture that was half shrug, half nod. "Family from Detroit. Gave'em a minivan."

I smiled. "Historic triangle, Busch Gardens, or Civil War memorials?"

He shrugged and picked up a copy of Sports Illustrated he

kept under the counter. "Don't know. Don't care."

I wanted to tell him to do something besides stand there, but the truth was we were a tight ship. We filed everything right away, kept things well-ordered, had a cleaning lady come in every night to spruce things up and keep the tiles their whitest.

An airport shuttle pulled up and a couple stepped off, a woman in an Ally McBeal knock off suit and stiletto heels. The guy wore a dark suit and designer sunglasses and gave me one of those chin jerks that is supposed to be a nod. I head jerked back at him. "Good morning," I said.

"Need a sports car." He smiled. The woman acted bored and drummed her fingers on the counter. I pegged them as business associates and bed partners. She wore a wedding ring. He didn't. Not my business, but I always liked to speculate anyway.

My cell phone pinged, so I gestured for Brent to take over and I stepped to the back to answer.

"Hello?"

"It's time. I told you it was going to be soon. I need you to come and get me." Madeline was puffing out short breaths, the breathy huffs were loud in my ears.

"How far apart are the contractions?"

"I don't know. Seven minutes? Five? Just get here."

I hung up and gestured for Brent to step away from the couple.

"Madeline is in labor," I said.

"Cool. Congrats, man. Go on. I got it here."

"Yeah. Look. I need you to get that Tahoe to the right guy today. He's a VIP and he wants that car."

"The one under the maple?"

"Yeah. Look. Make sure he gets it." I laid the Winstons on the counter. "Put these in the glove box."

"Fine." He turned back to the couple.

I grabbed his arm. "Brent, listen. It is very important that car goes to the right customer. Do you understand?"

"Yes. Geez. I got it. Tahoe. Tree shit. Right guy. Go. Have a baby. I've got work to do."

I stood there for a minute, wondering how angry Madeline would be if I waited until the Tahoe was off the lot before picking her up. Brent was back at the counter with the couple, his head bent over the paper forms I still hadn't gotten around to computerizing yet. The Tahoe was where it was supposed to be, Brent would make sure the smokes were in the glove box, and Madeline was in labor. Shit.

I walked back outside, climbed into my car, and drove toward home.

4
BRENT

Clyde left in a hot panic. Can't say I blame him. I can't even believe he had space in his head for some special reservation when his wife is in labor, but I guess if it were my name on the business, I'd want everything to go right, too.

Before the dust even settled from Clyde's sprint out the door, the Griffin family came back. Same dumpy Midwestern foursome pulling their same beige luggage and their same fat asses. This couldn't be good.

"Mr. Griffin, you're back," I said, trying to be cheery before the shit storm I knew was coming my way.

"That car you rented me," he said. "It smells." Then he added, "Bad," in case I thought he'd come back to compliment us on the floral scent of our air fresheners. We don't use air fresheners. You get what you get.

"I'm so sorry about that."

"Smells like ass," the boy said. His mother immediately shushed him with a small slap to the back of the head. I could see the embarrassment on her face for her son and her husband. I could imagine the argument in the van before turning around, her all, "It's fine, just drive," and him all, "I won't pay for a car that smells like ass."

"We want a new one," he said. He stuck out his chin, such as it was, and acted entitled. I took a deep breath, working hard to keep it together.

"Of course. No problem." I sounded less like a smiley glad hand and more like a waiter about to go back to the kitchen and spit in his food. I checked the roster of vehicles, of which there aren't many on our lot. No more minivans. "I'm afraid, Mr. Griffin," I started. I saw him already tense up, planning his rebuttal. "That was our last minivan."

"That's not my problem." His face glowed red and tiny beads of sweat dotted his forehead all the way back across his dome.

"The van you gave me smells like something died in the air conditioning unit and it's obvious someone was smoking in there. We specifically asked for a non-smoking car."

He hadn't, since that wasn't one of our options, but the customer is always right. Often times a humongous dick, but always right.

"Well," I said as I checked the list of cars. "I can give you a four door sedan."

"No, that won't do. We need the storage. Can you not see the bags we have with us?"

"Sean...," his wife tried to calm him down, but not trying very hard in case he turned his anger on her. She knew the drill.

"No, Linda, we won't be treated like this. This is our vacation. I'm not driving around in a car that smells like a public toilet and I'm not driving around in some Japanese shoebox. We're from goddamn Detroit for Christ sake."

"Kids, you come with me," Linda said as she ushered the kids away from Daddy's tantrum.

I balled up my fists, let them loose again and tried talking myself out of using them on this jerk wad. I promised Clyde I wouldn't have another incident like that again. The last guy I punched sued us. Almost won too, if he hadn't been drunk. After that, Clyde installed the security camera, but I think that was as much to check up on me than any rude customers.

"I want that one," he said. He pointed a fat finger at the black Chevy Tahoe I hadn't had a chance to move yet.

"I do have an SUV you can have, Mr. Griffin. Let me just get it from around back and run it through the washer—"

"I want that one." God, throw a diaper on this guy and he'd be a three hundred pound baby.

"That one is already reserved."

"Again, not my problem. You said you had another one, give it to them. I've already been delayed enough. I'm not going to sit around your shitty airport while you wash another stink bomb of a car when a perfectly good, clean one is right fucking there."

I saw the mom put a hand over one of each kid's ears.

I wanted to punch this guy more than I've ever wanted to punch someone before in my life, but not more than I wanted to keep my job, so fuck it. Let him have the damn thing. The sooner he left, the sooner I could wash up the other Tahoe and give Clyde's special repeat customer guy a twin of the Tahoe outside.

"You're right," I said. The thing they all want to hear. "I'll change the paperwork for you, no need to sign anything else. You have a nice day." I lifted the keys from the desk where Clyde had set them and traded Mr. Griffin for the minivan keys, then I secretly wished for the Tahoe to blow a tire, run off into a ditch, catch fire and trap him and his fat fucking family inside the burning wreckage where they could all sizzle to death like the chubby little sausage links they were.

I smiled the whole time I handed over the keys, but as soon as he turned his back I gave him the finger. I made sure the security camera could see it.

5
SEAN

Linda glared at me the whole time I lugged the bags into the back of the Tahoe. She sat on her butt in the passenger seat, looking over the heads of Chad and Becky, and glared at me. The car was clean, the air conditioner worked, and it didn't smell like bunghole. How about a "Thank you, Sean?" Or even a "Nice job, honey?" Or maybe just not being a bitch? I closed the hatch and popped another antacid. I didn't want to tell Linda about the upset stomach. She might think I was having a heart attack and make me detour to the ER. Or maybe not, I thought as I climbed into my seat and drove off the lot.

After a few minutes, when she realized I wasn't going to look back at her and engage in the usual passive aggressive argument, she faced forward, put her sunglasses on, and read the regional map.

The kids plugged themselves into their iPods and stared out their windows.

"Get onto I-64," Linda said, even though it was obvious that was the road we had to take to get to Colonial Williamsburg.

The phone in my pocket buzzed, but I didn't take it out to check. My chest twinged a little bit. Guilt? Fear? Both? I didn't know. Originally I felt justified by what I'd done, how I'd used some creative accounting to finance our vacation—a vacation long overdue because my raise was longer overdue.

My job was flipping homes. Or, more realistically, buying the abandoned structures in Detroit, knocking them down and scrapping out the lumber, the cabinets, the copper piping, and anything else we could salvage. Problem was, even though the business was my idea, my plan, my ambition, the financing came from my older brother, Ken, and two of his banker friends.

Funny how over the last three years they made a mint and I barely made enough to feed my kids and my wife and hang onto my vintage 1981 split entry modular home, complete with olive green refrigerator and stove. I was supposed to receive a bonus of no less than fifty K for the last three years, and for the last three years I got nothing. No bonus. No raise. Just more work on the endless stream of abandoned homes.

In December I asked Ken about a raise or at least a bonus. "No can do, Sean. Wish I could, but the partners...you know how it is." He said it like I was supposed to understand that it was okay to screw someone out of an idea, out of a dream.

Linda said I should get a lawyer out of the yellow pages and get one of those free consultations. I nodded, like maybe it was a good idea. Linda likes to be right and my job is to let her think she is. So when she asked me a few days later how the meeting with the lawyer went I told her it went fine and that Ken had agreed to pay me more money, that we would be going on a vacation.

Don't know why I said it. Don't know why I started stealing from the company and selling stuff on the side under the radar. I know right from wrong. I know good from bad. I also know my brother and his two friends screwed me and, as the saying goes, one good screw deserves another.

Sure, I'd go back and face the music. I'd have to eventually, but for now I was going to take my family on a much needed, much deserved vacation.

"Don't forget we need to be in Virginia Beach by nine o'clock tonight for a late cookout with my parents."

Oh yeah, did I mention part of the vacation was spending a weekend with Linda's folks? I called it penance and looked for a place to pull off for a drink. I was going to need something stronger than diet soda to get through the day.

6
SKEETER

It was too fuckin' long since I had a bump of anything. Even a thin rail would do to keep my head clear. Smoke it, snort it, stick it up my ass—doesn't matter none to me when I'm feeling the chill. But I felt worse. Must have been sittin' around that shitty airport again that made me want a little something-something. Must have been knowing I had another run for Corgan that wouldn't get me no closer to movin' up out of the delivery boy business.

Must have been a hundred runs I done for him. Barely scored me a discount on the crystal. No point talkin' about no respect. I'd have to do ten thousand runs 'fore that happened, looked like. Corgan was just gonna sit up in his big-ass Annandale house and keep sending me down to the corner store for smokes. What it felt like anyway.

It was a fuck ton of responsibility, those runs. I don't think he realized. He'd been up in the suburbs too long, forgot what it's like in the trenches.

Well, fuck it. The hours were good enough, even though the eight in the morning shit was a little tiresome. Checking the clock I was a little late. Served them fuckin' right for settin' it up so early.

Shaking off the bone deep need for a bump of crystal, I cracked my neck, wedged a pinch of Skoal in my lip, and finished my walk from the airport shuttle station to the rental car place—my own car having been stashed in an out-of-the-way location to be retrieved later, after the delivery was made.

The morning was just starting to heat up and the sun felt good on my arms. If I can help it, I don't do sleeves. I must have sent five hundred innocent pairs of sleeves to the garbage chute. I had enough tats to make you do a double take to see if I was wearing sleeves anyway, but whatever tight-assed fuck invented sleeves a hundred years ago or whatever, he can suck my dick.

Jean vest over sleeveless T from the last Slipknot show I went to. Jeans and Chuck T's. You see me coming and you might not run away, but you'll grab your pocketbook a little tighter to you.

Just the way I like it.

They had one of those stupid bells over the door. I never got tired of making fun of them for that. Almost as much fun as a guy named Clyde naming his goddamn business after himself. You got a name of Clyde and you run the hell away from that shit. You don't fucking advertise it.

I go by Skeeter. Why? 'Cause my shit-ass stupid parents named me Leslie. Don't see me on TV with an ad for Leslie's drug courier and general mule services, do you?

Only Clyde wasn't here.

"The fuck are you?" I asked the yokel behind the counter.

"I'm Brent. How may I help you?" He gave me a smile and I knew he was thinking he wanted me to eat a bag of dicks. I didn't give a fuck. I didn't have no fucks to give.

"Clyde here?"

"He had to step out. His wife's in labor. Are you here for the Tahoe?"

"Yeah. I'm here for the Tahoe."

"Okay," he said and he turned to get a set of keys. "Let me just run it through the wash for you—"

"The fuck do I care if it's got bird shit on it?"

That stopped him in his tracks. "It's just company policy to—"

"Don't care. Keys." I held out my hand, spiderweb palm tattoo ready to snare the keys.

This Brent guy knew better than to fuck with me. He shrugged his shoulders, set the keys in my hand, says, "Clyde said all the paperwork is already taken care of."

"Fuckin' better be." I turned and head for the door. "Thanks, Fucko."

Hey, Corgan. I got your pack of smokes. I'll be there soon. Can I polish your shoes for you next? Maybe suck your dog's dick? Anything you want, sir.

Fuckin' Corgan.

7
BRENT

That guy was a repeat customer? A VIP? What a douche.

The guy smelled like a jockstrap, had meth-head teeth, and I swear I saw lice in his hair. I really hoped he didn't get that shit in our car. It's so expensive to get them out. You have to get the whole interior steam cleaned, and even with that there's like a ten percent chance it won't get them all.

Sometimes it was easy to forget Virginia was still the start of redneck country. Who else chewed tobacco in this day and age? It's a big state and we're not all lobbyists and government contractors. Dirt bags who haven't yet slid down to the Carolinas still populate our state like possums. I only wished as many turned up dead on the side of the highway. Especially when they're rude assholes like that guy.

Whatever. I knew Clyde had been into some stuff on the side. Rentals with no paperwork, all mysteriously taken care of by Clyde personally. Special cars, always big SUVs, reserved for weeks ahead of time. His business, not mine. The cars always came back. I always got paid.

Shit, speaking of which, if Clyde was off at the hospital all day having a baby, I was starting to think this might not be payday.

8
SKEETER

Maybe I was too hard on the dude. Nah, fuck him. Piece of shit minimum wage jockey. Aw, hell, I didn't even know the guy. I needed to start to give people a little more room to be the douche bags they were and stop judging them so damn much. I did that thing where I talk to myself inside my head. I do it a lot. I said: Skeeter, you need to level out. 'Course a bump of the good stuff sure woulda helped.

See? The government is trying to keep drugs illegal, when it really makes me a much better citizen. Probably woulda helped me find that goddamn car, too.

Finally found it round the side baking in the hot sun. I thought Clyde knew enough to park it in the shade. I hated to think what would befall him if some of the shipment got cooked up in the ceiling.

I stood looking at it, saying to myself: If that's what they consider a dirty car, what the hell would they say about mine? Not that I saw her very much anymore with all these deliveries. Felt like I was back in jail and missin' my baby. I shoulda started writing her letters. I wonder if my Honda can only read Japanese?

Maybe after this one I could take a fuckin' break. The big score, Corgan's sidecar said. That brown-nosing shit eater, Dell. Corgan would never let anything slip about the size or value of a shipment, but his goddamn Siamese twin did. Dell was so far up Corgan's ass sometimes, I bet he'd got the place furnished.

Dell said this was a double load. Then he slipped and said triple a little later. Once again, pays to get a little powder up someone's nose. Like a truth serum.

I gotta say, for so many bricks of coke sewn into the roof lining of that Tahoe, it looked like a normal goddamn vehicle. I guess that's what we paid this Clyde yahoo for. He was good at what he did, I'll give him that. Or at least he had a good seamstress.

But would it kill the guy to make an appearance at his own drug deal? I mean, I guess it wasn't a deal, just a delivery, but I bet if Corgan showed up he'd have been here. But when it's lowly ol' Skeeter? I get the temporary help. The fuck did I expect from someone named Clyde.

Serious though, this ceiling was smooth as a car right off the lot. Too smooth. I ran my hand along the top and I should have felt them, right? Thirty-three bricks. I'd feel them no matter how nice they stitched up the panels after they stuffed them up in there, right?

This didn't feel right. Fuck it. I was going in. Nothing a little buck knife wouldn't fix. And if Corgan wanted to get uppity about a little slash in the roof, I'd explain how I was just making sure his merchandise was all where it was supposed to be.

Which it wasn't. I got foam, I got metal from the roof panel. I got no drugs.

Oh, Clyde, Clyde, Clyde. Thought you could fool ol' Skeeter, did ya?

9
BRENT

The little dirt bag with the attitude and no sleeves came back. I silently wished for the fat-ass Griffin family.
He pushed the door open so hard I thought the glass might break. Then he let out a bad Ricky Ricardo impression.
"Loooooo-seee. You got some 'splain' to do."
"Is there a problem?"
He lifted his hand fast and flashed me a fixed blade knife in his hand. He looked like he might fling it my direction like we were in carnival. He pulled back his chapped lips and showed me his dark stained teeth, slammed the keys I'd just given him down with his non-knife wielding hand.
"Where is it, motherfucker?"
"The car? It's...it's..." I scrambled on the desk for the paperwork with the space number for the Tahoe. It should have been easy to find, being the only SUV left in the lot. And our lot wasn't very big to begin with.
"Not the car, asshole. What's in the car. Or what's not in the car."
In the car but not in the car? What?
"I...I don't know what—"
He drove the knife down into the counter. The tip cut through the speckled green enamel top and a snowflake pattern of cracks flashed out around it. I pushed back in my rolling chair until it hit the wall behind me.
"Look, shitbag, I get it. You ain't the man in charge. I ain't either. But we both got a job to do and neither one of us wants to get our boss on the phone, right?"
My boss. Clyde. He officially doesn't pay me enough for this kind of crap.
"I don't know what you're talking about."
He leaned over the counter, stretching a skinny arm twined with tattoos at me and pointed over my shoulder. On his arm I

picked out a topless lady in a hula skirt, a snake wrapped around a flaming skull and what I swear was a swastika, but that one looked homemade—or prison made probably.

"That car out there is empty," he said. "I need it to be full."

"The gas tank?"

He rolled his eyes and let out an exaggerated sigh. "Not the fucking gas tank." He turned and spit on the floor. "You really don't know your asshole from your elbow, do you?"

"I sure as hell don't know what you're talking about, sir." When in doubt, be professional.

The guy grabbed his knife, plucked it out of the counter, and stashed it away in whatever sheath he had up under his jean vest.

"I really did have better fuckin' things to do today, y'know?"

Then he turned on his heels and went out the door, pulling a cell phone as he went. The Tahoe keys stared at me from the counter. I debated whether to call Clyde first or go look in the car and try to figure out what the hell wasn't there that the guy wanted.

10
SKEETER

I swear to fucking god you want something done right...I don't even know what. I tell you one thing though—I was not about to take the fall for thirty-three missing bricks of coke. That was one of those times when I'm glad to just be a messenger boy. I hoped to fucking Christ on the cross that Corgan didn't want to shoot the messenger.

So, on second thought, I killed the phone call. Decided on calling this Clyde jackass. Let him deal with it. I'd put him on the phone with Corgan to break the news. Let Corgan kill that messenger. Let him kill the whole goddamn U.S. Postal Service, as long as it wasn't me.

I thought: So, okay, Clyde. Let's hear what you've got to say for yourself.

11
CLYDE

I got back to the house in a record ten minutes and heard Madeline screaming from the driveway. I looked up and down the street to see if anyone was listening, sort of embarrassed, sort of excited. My kid was about to be born. Madeline was going to give birth. It was a crazy feeling and for a second I didn't know what to do. I stood there in the driveway and paced around a little bit before pulling it together and heading inside.

My phone rang just as I opened the door and was about to let her know I was home.

"Hello?"

"What the fuck, asshole?" It was Skeeter. Madeline stood in the kitchen, her arms braced on the counter, blowing through a contraction.

I lowered my voice as I ducked back into the foyer out of her line of sight. "Excuse me?" I said into the phone.

"Where the fuck is the shit?"

"Nice language, douche bag. It's where I put it." My chest felt heavy and I rested my hand on the wall.

Madeline poked her head around the corner. "Get the goddamn bags," she said through clenched teeth, "and hang up that phone."

I held up a finger and stepped back out on to the porch. Skeeter sounded like he needed some of what was in the Tahoe. "It's not where you put it. I was just in the Tahoe and there's nothing there, man. Nothing."

I hadn't checked the Tahoe for the shipment. Shit, shit, shit. It was possible I was robbed last night, in which case I would have a hell of a time putting in a police report. I could just see myself calling the cops and telling them to be on the lookout for a car with a ceiling full of dope. "Shit. Okay. Let me call Brent and see what's going on."

"Brent? Is that the asshole running the shop right now?"

Madeline appeared in the doorway, doubled over. "Get...off...the...goddamn...phone."

I held up my finger again and she looked like she wanted to bite it off. "Look. Let me call him," I said to Skeeter. "There's something wrong. Your car was ready to go."

"Yeah. You call him," Skeeter said, and the line went dead.

I leaned over and rested my hands on my knees while I tried to catch my breath. When I looked up, Madeline was gone from the doorway. I found her inside lugging her overnight case down the hallway. "You're an asshole," she said, pushing past me.

I took the bag from her and held her elbow, guiding her to the car.

I got her settled, strapped her in and sped to the hospital, which was five minutes away. I kept my cell clutched in my hand but didn't dare dial. Madeline already wasn't speaking to me and I didn't know what the hell to say to her. All I could think of was that I was going to kill Brent if Corgan didn't kill me first.

I filled out the forms for admission, which we had actually pre-filled two weeks earlier in order to streamline the process. So much for that. A nurse helped Madeline into a wheelchair and whisked her away to labor and delivery. I watched them turn into a room down the hall and waved that I'd be right there. Madeline scowled at me.

I pulled out my phone and dialed Brent. His voice was shaky when he picked up. "Hello?"

"I'll give you sixty seconds to tell me how bad you fucked things up, Brent, and then I'll give you ten seconds to tell me why I shouldn't kill you."

12
BRENT

First I got attitude from the VIP dirt bag, then I got an earful from Clyde. It was starting to feel like my last day on the job; still to be determined if I left by my own volition or by getting fired. Clyde sure didn't sound any too pleased with my performance.

"Is this about the guy with the SUV?" I asked.

"Of course it is, Brent. Skeeter's fucking pissed." Clyde did a lousy job of hiding his rage. Stress I'd gotten used to from Clyde, even a few outbursts of raised tone or short temper, but even in the changes I'd been witnessing for the last few months, this was over the top.

"Where the fuck is the car?" he asked.

"I gave it to him," I said. "Wait? Did you say the guy's name is Skeeter?"

He ignored me. "Well, he's saying it's not the right one."

"Who is? Skeeter? Is that for real?"

"He's goddamn real, Brent. And you don't want to piss him off."

Pissing people off seemed to be my specialty for the day. "What's the damn difference. They're both Tahoes."

He paused. "What do you mean, they're both Tahoes?"

I sighed. Not even nine a.m. and I'd had my fill of crappy attitude for the whole day, plus tomorrow. "I mean we had two on the lot, identical. One guy doesn't like one, the other guy doesn't like the other. I can't win."

"What other guy, Brent?" Clyde sounded desperate, like if I was in the same room with him he'd have slapped me across the face. I'd definitely quit then.

"The fat guy from Detroit with the family."

"You're saying you gave him the Tahoe?"

"I gave him a Tahoe."

Clyde muttered a few barely audible holy shit, holy shit, holy shits to himself. "That wasn't just a Tahoe, Brent. That was the Tahoe. You've fucked me. Royally fucked me."

"Well, how the hell was I supposed to know?"

Clyde exploded. "Because I told you!" He got control of his volume, sounded like he cupped a hand over his mouth and the phone. "I told you which car to give to the guy and you gave it away."

"What's the damn difference?"

"I can't talk about this now. I need to make a phone call."

Clyde clicked off the line. I felt sorry, honestly sorry, if I'd screwed anything up, but to my knowledge I hadn't. And I felt I hadn't seen the last of Skeeter for the day.

13
CLYDE

I hung up the phone and swallowed the dry lump of shit in my throat. I was fucked. There was no way around it. Brent had fucked everything up, including me. I pocketed my phone and went in to hold Madeline's hand. She was sitting up on the bed, leaning forward, holding her knees and rocking. "The contractions are still about seven minutes apart," the nurse said, "but they seem to be causing her some pain. I'm going to get her a shot."

She brushed past me on the way out the door and Madeline's contraction seemed to end. She leaned back and gave me a weak smile. Her face softened a little. "Wow," she said. "You look like hell. I guess you must be pretty freaked out by this."

I was freaked out by Brent not parking the Tahoe where he was supposed to. I was freaked out by Madeline's mood swings. I was freaked out that I was probably never going to get to watch my kid grow up. I nodded. Yeah. I was pretty fucking freaked out. My collar was soaked with sweat. I didn't dare take off my jacket. I was drenched. I sat down beside the bed and she held my hand and gave it a little pat. "It will be okay, hon. We're gonna make great parents," she said. I kissed her fingers and nodded again. I needed to talk to Corgan. "Sorry about all the yelling," she said. I tried to give her a smile.

The nurse came back with a syringe and bustled around the room like I wasn't even there. She helped Madeline onto her side, talking the whole time. "Now, ideally we want to get an epidural in..."

"That'd be great," Madeline said.

"But the anesthesiologist is on another case right now, so we'll just have to wait." She swabbed Madeline's butt with an alcohol swab and gave her the injection. "So you'll just have to muddle along like they did in the past with just an injection to help you with the pain."

Madeline rolled her eyes at me and rolled onto her back as another contraction took hold. My phone buzzed in my pocket.

"You," the nurse snapped her fingers at me. "Sit here and help her through this. Just like the Lamaze classes."

The phone buzzed again and I knew it had to be Brent or Corgan. I sat beside Madeline and breathed with her, watching the door to the hallway with one eye and the nurse with the other. She continued to mill about the room for a minute before leaving. She straightened Madeline's sheets, brought her a damp cloth for her head and checked to make sure she had fresh ice chips. "You should really be the one doing this," she said, holding the cup of ice chips under my nose and shaking it. I wanted to answer, but there were too many other things to worry about besides an overbearing nurse who thought all men were shit. All I could think about was the phone in my pocket and Madeline squeezing the hell out of my hand.

The nurse left, the contraction passed, and I pretended I felt faint, which wasn't really too far from the truth. I said I needed the vending machine and walked out into the hallway. I bumped into a few people on my way to the waiting room. Once there, I pulled out my phone and punched Corgan's number.

"Clyde," he said as he picked up, his voice cheerful. Like nothing at all was wrong. "Beautiful day."

I tried to push words out from between dry lips. "Yeah."

There was a long pause while I waited for him to tell me I was already dead. "I've had words with Skeeter," he said. "I'd like to hear what you have to say."

I cleared my throat. "There's been a mistake," I said.

He laughed softly. I'd never met him, but I'd heard about what he was capable of. "Skeeter told me. Where's the car?"

"I don't know. Some family from Detroit."

"You don't know. Well, in that case, I suppose you better figure it out. If you have difficulty, I will be happy to provide you some motivation."

"Yessir." I didn't say anything else and neither did he. There was nothing more to say. I knew what would happen to me if I didn't get the car back.

14
BRENT

This time he did crack the glass. Nothing shattered or anything, but a fat crack ran up from the bottom to just below the push bar. Nearly broke the bell, too. That, plus the counter repair, made today a pretty expensive day for Clyde, I guess.

More pressing for me, was the sleeveless dirt bag—Skeeter according to Clyde—crossing the lobby toward me again. No knife this time, which I took as a good sign.

He slammed a hand over the keys, drew them back off the counter, staring at me the whole time.

"I'll be back," he said. Damn, this guy was a regular font of pop culture clichés.

I didn't say a word as he went back out and turned toward the back where the Tahoe still sat. I guess Clyde talked him into keeping it. All I knew was that I was damn glad to see him go, and I felt like I was starting to get more of an idea about how weird Clyde got when certain days came around, certain cars needed to be matched with certain drivers. Why he got all nervous.

It wasn't about the baby. Clyde was into something. Something illegal. Something I didn't want a damn thing to do with. Maybe I could go across to the airport and get a job as one of those guys with the orange glow sticks who guide the planes in. That could be fun.

No sleeveless a-holes would come harass you on the tarmac of an airport. Not like out here where anyone can treat you like shit on the heel of their boot and you have to sit and take it because the customer is always—

I heard the Tahoe before I saw it. When I did see it, the front grill was finishing the job of cracking the glass on the front door. This Skeeter guy had revved the engine and that big V-8 boosted all two thousand pounds of Detroit steel through the glass front of the rental lobby and smeared tire marks across our linoleum. I swear I heard the bell over the end-of-the-world smashing of glass and metal.

The engine growled like a lion freshly loose from the zoo. I'd never been in an enclosed space with a huge engine like that before and it reminded me of the jets taking off a few hundred yards away. I rolled my chair back into the wall and absurdly put up my hands as the SUV barreled forward in an explosion of glass and regional maps from the map rack he flattened on the way in.

The engine noise died down as he let off the gas and the front end of the Tahoe punched the tall counter separating me from the lobby, normally a welcome barrier between the stale sweat of businessmen just off a cross country flight, and now a lifesaving barricade between me and a crazy man in a rented car.

The sound came to an abrupt end as the last of the glass hit the floor and Skeeter twisted the key to shut off the engine. The counter leaned forward like it was ready to pounce on me. The pen-on-a-chain normally used for people to sign their contracts dangled in front of me and tapped against my kneecap as it swung in violent circles.

The lobby smelled of gasoline and transmission fluid, burnt rubber and freshly splintered wood. Skeeter opened the door, slid out and walked over the tilted counter like it was nothing more than some fallen timber in the woods; and I guess it was.

He dropped the keys in my lap, licked a line of blood trickling from his nose and spit on the floor again.

"This one's busted. I'll need a new one. Be back in two hours."

He snorted more blood back up his nose and turned away from me. I sat in stunned silence as he left me alone in my crumbling office. Yeah, I really started to doubt if I would get paid today.

My shoes crunched over the hail storm of broken glass in the lobby. The right taillight of the Tahoe still blinked as if Skeeter had only missed a tight right turn instead of intentionally plowing through the front window of the rental shop.

I got out my cell phone, doubting if the company phone still worked. Time to quit this job. Sorry for whatever you're mixed up in, Clyde, but this shit is above my pay grade. Maybe I could go work at Norfolk. Richmond airport is a ghetto, and from the looks of it the neighborhood was getting worse. No more impatient businessmen for me. No more liars trying to tell me the car only had a half tank of gas when they rented it. No more fat families treating me like a servant boy. And no more steel and glass death bombs crashing through the front aiming for my lap. I'm out.

I dialed Clyde. When he picked up he sounded like he was the one in labor.

"Brent, good, here's what I need you to do—"

I cut him off. "I quit."

"What?"

"Yeah, I quit. Screw this. That guy, Skeeter? He just drove a car through the lobby."

"He did what?"

I spoke slowly to emphasize my displeasure. "He drove. A car. Through the front. He almost crushed me, man. I still have glass in my hair. Seriously, I was almost a bug on the front grill, man."

"Calm down, Brent."

"Calm down?" I was about to tell him where he could shove his calm down, but Clyde seemed even more pissed off and stressed out than me. I wondered what almost crushed him.

"I need you to find that other Tahoe. The Detroit people. You need to find them and get the car back. Right away. Like, now."

"How the hell am I gonna do that?"

"Just do it."

Easy for him to say. "I'm not the cops, man. I can't put out an APB."

"No cops," Clyde blurted. "No cops at all. You didn't call the cops already, did you?"

"No." I'd had it with pussy footing around. Friend or no friend, Clyde's right to privacy had been revoked. "What the hell is going on, man?"

I heard distant hospital sounds between his heavy breathing.

"Seriously," I said. "You've been a mess for a few months now. I thought it was the baby, but now I want to know what it really is. Apparently I'm involved. And since I was the one who almost got killed by a meth head in a V-8 killing machine, I think I have a right to know before I go off and try to fix whatever problem I didn't know I started. A problem that, at the end of the day, is still your problem, dude."

He took a deep breath. His voice dropped to a low whisper, barely rising above the cell phone static on the line. I watched my reflection in the rear window of the Tahoe tinted in red blinking light as Clyde explained.

He was a drug runner. Apparently, so was I. I'd been handing over cars stuffed with bricks of cocaine and crystal meth and bundles of Oxycontin pills for weeks now. Clyde had them stitched into the lining of the ceiling panels and then driven out all across Virginia and down south. He had partners in baggage who unloaded the stuff from planes before it went through security, they got it to him, he put it in the cars, then Skeeter or sometimes another guy would come drive the car away and Clyde got paid. It all ran out of some big guy in the suburbs of D.C.

And now I gave away a Chevy Tahoe filled to the brim with the biggest load Clyde had ever worked with. He skirted around telling me how much it was worth, but if you have to ask...

I watched my face fall a little more each time the red light of the turn signal filled the room. A warning light.

"Holy shit, dude."

"Yeah," he sighed like he was finally unburdened. "Holy shit."

"So this Skeeter guy, he's just a driver?"

"Yeah. I already talked to the big man."

"And told him what?"

"That I would get the car back."

"You mean I would get the car back."

His anger had faded in the telling of the story. He sounded exhausted now. "Brent, I'm having a baby over here."

"Not my fault."

"But it is kinda your fault that you gave away the wrong car."

My blood heated up. I tried not to pop off. "He said it smelled. And the customer is always right."

"They'll kill me."

His bluntness threw me off for a second. I also had a stark realization. "And now they know who I am."

"I'm sorry, man."

I kicked a small pile of glass with the toe of my shoe, saw the fallen bell amid the debris. "I guess I'll try to get the car back."

"I'll help out any way I can. As soon as I can get away," he offered.

"If this thing goes south, I really don't want to take the fall for you."

"We get that car back and everything is fine again. I'll even cut you in this time."

I crunched back behind the tiled counter. "What about the other times? Free labor?"

"College fund for the kid."

"So if I ask for some of that, I'm stealing from a baby."

"Trust me, with this score, you won't be feeling shorted."

When did he start talking like a drug dealer? Goddamn, but I was between a rock and a bigger, meaner rock. And a guy named Skeeter.

"I still quit," I said.

"You can take a year off in style once we get it all back."

I dug through the trash behind the counter and found the Griffin family's paperwork under a pile of Busch Gardens brochures. "I'll make some calls."

15
SEAN

I pulled off the interstate in Williamsburg and stopped at a Waffle House. Everyone likes the food and it's pretty cheap. Linda still got that furrow in her brow though. She said, "It's our vacation. Couldn't you spring for IHOP?"

I climbed from the car without saying anything. Linda sat there for a minute and I could tell she was surprised. I felt a little bad. I mean, she didn't have any idea what was going through my head, what I had done. I couldn't tell her, not without a scene. And we were on our way to see her parents. I could only imagine how bad it would be if I told her and she told them.

We filed inside and Linda and the kids took a booth. I went to the men's room and stared at myself in the mirror. My cell phone, which had been surprisingly quiet, buzzed in my pocket. I pulled it out. Unknown number. I waited five minutes and then checked the voice mail.

"Uh hi. Mr. Griffin? This is Brent from Clyde McDowd Rentals? There seems to have been a misunderstanding. We gave you the wrong car. We have an identical one here for you. Would you please bring the vehicle back as soon as possible, like immediately? To compensate you, we would like to give you your rental entirely free of charge." His voice cracked the tiniest bit on the last sentence. I'm no idiot. He was nervous about something. Like maybe the cops were in the rental office trying to track me down. Well no thanks, mister. I'll just keep right on trucking if it's all the same to you.

I splashed some water on my face and pocketed my phone.

Linda had ordered me a coffee and a Coke, both of which sat at my place waiting for me. The kids were plugged into their iPods again. I slid in beside Chad. Linda raised an eyebrow at me. "Well?" she said.

"Well what?"

"Well. What's up your butt?"

"I just don't want to stay with your parents tonight. We still want to see Colonial Williamsburg…"

"Nobody else wants to see Colonial Williamsburg but you," Becky said.

Chad echoed her sentiment.

"My mom and dad are expecting us. They'll be upset if we don't go."

"Who cares?"

She got that look on her face that said I was a shithead. "I care. And so does my dad."

"Let's stay at a Holiday Inn tonight!" Becky said. "We could swim in the pool. Grandpa and Grandma don't have a pool."

Chad snorted. "And their house smells like a litter box."

Linda smacked the back of his head but I could tell she was softening a little bit.

The waitress showed up and took our orders. Linda excused herself to call her folks and Chad and Becky continued to listen to their music. My phone buzzed a couple more times. Each time I let it go to voice mail and each time it was the same kid from the rental place trying to get me to bring the car back.

Linda showed up after we had placed our orders and I could tell by the sour look on her face and the way she didn't talk to me that she told her parents we were going to spend the night in a hotel.

The waitress brought our food and we all dug in, careful not to talk to each other. Seemed like that was the way our family had been going for a while now…silence and annoyance. At least I had an excuse. All I could think of was the money I had taken. I couldn't eat and when everyone was done I asked the waitress to just give me a big to-go cup of coffee.

I spotted the security guard standing by the door while I waited for my coffee. Linda and the kids headed out and got settled in the Tahoe. I accepted my coffee and pushed through the door. The waitress was trying to say something to me, but I ignored her. My vision had narrowed to a tunnel with the guard at the end of it. I gave him a nod as I passed, forcing myself to keep a nice, easy pace as I made my way to the car. "Excuse me, sir." He had followed me out.

I turned and tried to keep down what little I did eat. I had my keys in one hand and the coffee in the other. I figured I could throw the coffee on the guy and then make a run for it. But then Linda and the kids would be dragged into this mess and I didn't want that. I didn't want that at all.

I gave him a smile and raised my coffee cup in a bit of a salute. "Officer," I said.

He smiled back and said, "The waitress was calling after you. You forgot to pay."

Linda had the window rolled down and looked out at me and the cop. "Sean. I can't believe you forgot to pay. I can't believe it. I'm sorry, Officer. We are honest people. We truly are."

Yeah. Honest. "Sorry about that. I guess I was distracted."

He looked over my shoulder at Linda and the kids and gave a sympathetic nod. "How old are your kids?" he asked me.

Linda, as usual, answered. "Becky is twelve and Chad is thirteen. Irish twins. That's why I'm so round. Been over a decade and I still haven't lost the weight." She laughed and the cop's smile turned uncomfortable.

He cleared his throat and said, "Okay, then. Get that bill paid, sir. I'd hate to have to arrest you."

The words hung there in the air and I wondered if he could see how fast my heart was beating. I felt its pounding everywhere, my eyeballs, my neck, my throat, my chest, my fingers. The whole world seemed to be pulsing, growing and shrinking intermittently. I gave him a tight smile and headed back in to pay.

16
SKEETER

Couldn't help thinking maybe I left too soon. Mighta been a good idea to take a finger or something to let the boy know I was serious. Nah, the ol' truck through the window gag oughta keep him in check.

I sat back in my piece of shit Honda eating McDonald's with a Big Gulp Mountain Dew. My sister's baby got Dew Mouth. One of the last things I heard from her. She sat around in that trailer park feedin' her kid—a damn baby not even two years old—them nipple bottles full of the Dew. When the kid's teeth came in, they were already rotted out. And she started getting little mouth sores from all the sugar, I guess, or the carbonation. Hell, even I know better than to give a baby that green piss. I sure do like it, though. But for me, compared to most of what I put in my body, Mountain Dew is more like its namesake. A crisp, clear mountain stream of purity.

When I finished musing on my dumb ass sister, I really thought twice about the guy back at the rental place. Dumb as a stick, sure, but I ain't no smarter than a bundle of three or four sticks myself, so I wouldn't put it past him to be bullshitting me.

Either way, waiting over near him where I could keep eyes on him seemed like the thing to do. I drove the six blocks back to the long row of rental companies all lined up like whores on a Friday night. I had to pass all the classy ones, the ones that could afford good implants like Hertz and Avis, past the barely legals like Enterprise, down to the end of the blocks where the trannys and needle addicts hung. Wasted skeletons willing to suck and fuck for a five spot. That's where Clyde McDowd Rentals lived. That's the whore I'd been set up with, and wouldn't you know, she pulled a switch on me. Or more like she gave me the clap with crabs on top. Some inglorious dick rot meant to shrivel my pecker right off my body. Might as well have, anyway, if Corgan don't get his shit back in a timely fashion.

When I pulled up to the dark end of the street, I saw the bright combination of colors I hate most in the world—red and blue. Cop lights. First one I saw was an airport cop. Didn't count. Then I saw some real cops and I slowed to a halt a half block away. Shit. Guess my little stunt there drew some unwanted attention.

17
BRENT

Goddammit. Dammit. Dammit.

I kept my vice grip tight around the set of keys I'd snagged from the ruin of the key locker behind the counter. As soon as I saw the first of those cherry lights in the parking lot, I crouched low and got the hell out of there.

With my phone calls to Griffin a bust—the fat fucker was ignoring me—I didn't want to get held up answering a bunch of questions for the cops. Plus Clyde said no police at all. And with what he told me had gone missing, I didn't feel entirely confident I could tell a convincing story to a bunch of uniformed officers. Police have always made me nervous. Any kind of uniform does. The crossing guards at school used to make me sweat. I have no idea why. I mean, my dad was an Air Force officer, wore a uniform every day. He kept it on at dinner and didn't even bother to take it off when he whipped my ass for whatever nonsense thing I did wrong for the day.

Oh, wait. I think I just figured out why I hate uniforms...

I opened my palm to see what car I'd drawn in the lottery. My skin was indented with a ragged line where the rough edge of the key dug into my palm. The logo on the key was for the Infiniti, our one luxury car. Clyde thought it would be a good idea to have at least one on the list for the more upscale business travelers. We'd rented it out a grand total of three times and two of those were given away as free upgrades for people Clyde was trying to woo as repeat customers.

The good news for me is that we kept that car on the far edge of our row of spaces, almost into the Alamo lot. I could get there and start it up without being noticed, then drive out through the Alamo exit.

I reached the car with little trouble. I kept throwing glances over my shoulder at the growing party of cops in front of the wreck. They were all so fascinated by the scene, nobody ever looked my way.

I unhooked the single chain dividing our lot from theirs so I could drive over into the freshly painted lines of the Alamo rows of cars. Their asphalt was newer too, a deep black whereas ours was a dull gray with cracks and fine lines like an old lady's face pre-surgery. I rolled the car quietly into their lot and kept it at idle so the already quiet engine wouldn't make any more noise. When I got to the exit I waved at Jed, the booth guy. His job is to double check the paperwork before he lets you pass. He sits in a bright blue hut the size of a closet you'd complain about if it was in your house and he plays reggae music from a tiny boom box with damaged speakers. We'd talked on several occasions. Mostly when I wanted to buy some weed. I mean, you hear reggae music all day long and you kind of assume...well, I was right.

"Hey, Jed," I said, waving.

His bearded face turned to the light show of cops, then back to me. "Trouble over there?"

"Nothing our boys in blue can't handle."

He turned and looked again. I could tell he was curious, who wouldn't be? Not curious enough to leave the hut, though. A spaceship would have to land for that to happen. And it would have to be a pretty bad-ass spaceship.

I hoped he couldn't see the sweat on my upper lip or my forehead. "So, they don't want me to use our driveway, so could you just let me out over here?"

"What happened?"

I did not feel like shooting the breeze right then. I felt like changing my name and running for the border.

"Disgruntled customer," I said.

He turned and looked at the destruction again. "Boy, I guess."

"Can you just lift the gate, Jed, and I'll be on my way."

"What did you say to him that made him so mad?"

My anxiety level spiked. I felt trapped and I honestly considered if the Infiniti could make it through the wooden gate without causing too much noise so I could skip Jed and just get the hell away from there. Jed was into drugs, herbal ones at least, so maybe he would understand that every second I sat talking to him was another second a car load of dope was speeding away in the roof of a fat man's rental car, and if I didn't get it back, Clyde would be dead and probably me too.

Thinking it didn't help my anxiety.

"I don't know, Jed. Just one of those assholes I guess. Seriously though, could you?"

I motioned with my hand a raising the gate movement. He rotated on his spinning stool and he reminded me of an animatronic President you see at Monticello or whatever the hell George Washington's place is called. Slow, deliberate and almost on the verge of human.

"Sure man," he said. His hand paused over the button to my freedom. "You okay? Like, you hurt or anything?"

"I'm fine. Just want to get the hell out of here." I tried appealing to his nature. "Go home, y'know, smoke a bowl."

A smile lifted the left side of his mouth, showing a few white teeth through the black nest of whiskers. "I hear you, man."

He set me free. I gunned the engine a little too much and let go a short chirp of tires, but nothing to alert the cops. I turned right, back up the street past all the better known, undamaged rental companies. I passed by a little Honda two-door and I swear I saw Skeeter behind the wheel.

Great. Now I have PTSD and I'm seeing ghosts from my past traumas. Fantastic.

18
CLYDE

Madeline had my knuckles smashed together, and I could feel my wedding ring digging into the skin of my fingers. Between the sweat on my head and the sweat on hers, it was hard to tell which one of us was in labor.

The turbo-bitch nurse sauntered in to see how far along things were. "You look worse than your wife," she said. "You step out while I check Madeline over. If you faint on my floor, you won't be any good to anybody. I have plenty of legitimate patients to take care of."

She was moving me toward the door as she spoke, nudging me along with a gut that stuck out only slightly farther than her bosom. Her shoes squeaked loudly as she walked, pushing me along. I backed up, not wanting to argue with her. When Madeline cried out in pain, I froze, not wanting to abandon my wife, but wanting more than anything to call Brent and see if he had gotten hold of the guy who took the SUV. "Can't she have an epidural or something?" I asked. "There's got to be something you can do for her."

"Childbirth hurts, sir. We're taking good care of her." She had nudged me into the hallway and now stood with her bulk wedged in the doorway, blocking my view of Madeline. "The anesthesiologist is busy right now. Your wife is next on the list."

"Jesus Christ. You only have one anesthesiologist?"

She narrowed her eyes at me. "We employ four, but only two do epidurals and they're both busy. And I don't like your tone." She pushed the door closed.

I stepped back into the hallway and swiped a hand over my face. Behind the door, the nurse's muffled voice rasped and Madeline's softer voice answered. I took a deep breath and headed to the bathroom. Other men stood in the hallway of the labor and delivery wing, mostly dads-to-be emerging from the locker room nervously waiting to be summoned back inside to watch their wives deliver. Two men in suits leaned against the wall, arms and ankles crossed. I felt a little chill as I walked past them, but told myself it was nothing. The bathroom was empty and I moved into the stall farthest to the back to punch in Brent's number.

"Yeah," he said, sounding irritated.

"Where are you?"

"Driving. Where are you?"

Christ, he was gonna be dead when I saw him next. "Where are you driving, jackass?"

"I don't fucking know, Clyde. Guess I'm going to head to Williamsburg to try to find the fucking car you've got stuffed with drugs."

His voice rose on the last part of what he said and I could tell he was nervous. I swiped a hand down my face. Outside my stall, the bathroom door opened. I held my breath. Road noise from Brent's end of the line whooshed in my ear. Footsteps crossed the bathroom tile and I could tell there were two pairs of wingtips headed my way.

"You there, man? I'm going to Williamsburg. I figure that's my best bet. The kids were asking about Busch Gardens."

"Shh," I managed to breathe in the phone.

"What the fuck, Clyde? Go fuck yourself." He disconnected.

I guess Brent had had enough of me for the time being. I'd call him back if I lived through the next few minutes. The steps drew nearer. One set of shoes entered the stall next to mine. The other set stood right outside my stall door, toes pointing my direction.

"Come on out, Clyde McDowd," the voice beside me said.

19
SEAN

I found a Holiday Inn, just like the kids demanded. I pulled into the lot and looked for a place to park. In the backseat, Chad and Becky were arguing over whose butt was bigger, Beyonce's or J. Lo's. They had reached that level of shout that makes all fathers threaten to pull over. I wanted to shout out that no one's ass was big when compared to the size of their mother's, but that sort of comment is what makes a wife completely willing to testify against her husband in court.

I could see it now, Yes, Judge. He stole all that money and I knew nothing about it. And do you know what he was doing with it? Taking us to see my parents. Cheap-ass bastard never even offered to take me out of the country.

The judge would explain that this wasn't the point, that the money was stolen and her husband had broken the law. Linda would say, I understand that, your honor, and she'd say it just like that, just like he was something she had stepped in on the sidewalk, I'm trying to give you insight into his character. The selfish bastard couldn't even steal without being cheap about it.

So I let the kids yell at each other about ass size and kept my mouth shut. I put the car in park, rolled down the windows and switched the car off.

"What the hell are you doing?" Linda yelled over the kids.

My head hurt, and I hadn't stopped sweating for over an hour. I was fat, sure, but even a fat guy shouldn't sweat this much. She had to suspect something, something other than my glands, which I had blamed since the age of fourteen. I wanted a shower. I wanted out of this car. I wanted her dead. I supposed I needed to tell her; I KNEW I needed to tell her. She might be less surprised when state troopers hauled me off in handcuffs. She might have a story prepared for the kids.

OVER THEIR HEADS

"What the hell are you doing?" she asked. Actually, she yelled. Linda was what one would call a "yeller."

"I'm parking the fucking car," I shouted back.

20
CLYDE

I opened the stall door and found myself standing face to face with one of the suits. The second suit emerged from his stall. The outer door opened and a young dad-to-be poked his head in.

"Beat it," one of the suits said. The door shut and I was alone.

Stall guy moved over toward the sink and the guy in front of me nudged me along after him. I found myself in front of the mirror, my junk pressed against the counter, one guy on either side of me. I looked at the three of us, me and them. One suit wore a pale blue tie, the other a pale purple tie. Other than that, they looked enough alike to make me wonder if they were brothers...or clones.

"Let's go for a walk," Blue Tie said.

We moved through the door and out into the hallway.

Blue Tie held my right arm and Purple Tie held my left. We were just a group of guys wandering through the maternity ward in no big hurry. Never mind that one of us was sweating. Or crying. Maybe I was doing both. I had no idea.

Madeline's nurse was at the nurse's station as we passed, and she leaned over, resting on her meaty elbows as I walked by. She arched one eyebrow in a way that said she knew it all along. She knew I was no good and she couldn't wait until I was out of earshot to tell anyone who would listen.

I had no idea what she would tell Madeline. I had no idea if I'd see my kid. And I had to wonder if it was all worth it. Was any of it worth it? I thought about falling on the floor and peeing myself, pretending I had a seizure or something. Would these goons just run away or would they pick me up and carry me to their car and beat the shit out of me? Probably beat the shit out of me. Of course, that was bound to happen anyway the way things were headed.

I stayed where I was, held up between them, being pushed and dragged some, but mostly walking under my own steam, toward the elevator.

Inside, Purple Tie punched in a number on his phone. No doubt talking to Corgan. "We've got him." Anything else he said was lost because my own phone buzzed in my pocket. The sound was too loud in the elevator.

"Answer it," Blue Tie said.

I pulled it out. Brent. "Yeah," I said. My voice sounded like an old man's.

"I'm in Williamsburg. I just parked over by the Duke of Gloucester Street and walking past the Barnes and Noble."

Blue Tie took the phone from me and pushed the speaker button. Purple Tie said, "Hang on a second. We got some info on the other phone." He put his phone on speaker and held it out to my phone so now we were all just one big conference call. The elevator door opened and a woman carrying a bunch of balloons moved to step in.

"Fuck off," Blue Tie said. He said it real soft so it wouldn't pick up on the phone. The woman backed out and the doors slid closed.

"You there or what?" Brent voice crackled from the phone.

Blue Tie nudged me in the arm, like I should talk to him. I cleared my throat. "Any sign of the guy with our SUV?" I lowered my voice a little, tried to sound tough or at least like someone who wasn't about to piss in his pants.

Brent gave a snort. "No sign of him, man. And this place is busy. I can't believe the shit you got me into. I'm going to make one circuit here and if I find him you better hold onto your promise and cut me in."

My gut clenched. Purple Tie arched an eyebrow and the corners of his mouth lifted up. Brent hung up and Blue Tie handed my phone back to me.

Purple Tie put his phone to his ear and listened for a minute then disconnected and put it in his pocket. The elevator doors slid open and we pushed outside, into the front parking circle of the hospital. We walked across the street and into an ocean of cars. A strip mall hovered in the distance. It was the usual type of place for Virginia. Tattoo parlor, sushi joint, donut shop, tanning salon. We approached the strip mall and the suit twins nodded at the apron-clad owner of the sushi joint sweeping the sidewalk in front of his restaurant. He nodded once and then took his broom and went inside. The three of us moved around back.

Purple Tie pulled out his phone again and punched some numbers. When Corgan answered, the phone was put on speaker.

"Hello, Mr. McDowd," the voice sounded grainy. "You lost my shipment."

Blue Tie pulled back and punched me in the gut. I dropped to my knees but Purple Tie, holding the phone in one hand, used his other to hoist me back up again. Blue Tie took his jacket off.

"It was a mistake," I managed. "Brent—" I was cut off with another punch to my gut, a fist to the eye and an upper cut to my chin. I ended up on the ground again and tried to hear through the ringing in my ears.

"Is this 'Brent' the person you are now offering to cut in on your payment?"

I pushed myself to my knees, head bent as I tried to get my bearings. Blood dripped from my mouth onto the concrete. "It's not what you think," I said, looking up. Blue Tie seemed even bigger without his jacket on.

"What I think," the voice crackled, "is that it sounds like you don't need as big of a cut. So let's do this. You get my shipment back. File the insurance on your little business. We'll give you half of the original price."

"Half." My mouth went dry.

"Since you don't need as much, we won't give as much."

I blew out the breath I had been holding. They were going to let me live.

Purple Tie hoisted me up again while Blue Tie examined his knuckles and moved to put his jacket back on.

"Thank you, sir," I said. "Thank you."

"If you don't find my shipment and return it to me unharmed, I will make sure your wife and child suffer greatly before they die. Now you run along and find my drugs."

And that was all. Purple Tie punched the phone and put it in his pocket.

"I'd hurry if I were you," Blue Tie said. "We're going to head back to the hospital now and see how your wife is doing. She was looking pretty tired."

"Yeah," Purple Tie said. "Labor can really be hard."

"You fuckers," I said, lunging for Purple Tie. He easily side-stepped me and Blue Tie landed a punch to my ribs that dropped me again to my knees. They left, and as soon as I was able, I stood and made my way to my car.

21
BRENT

I knew I couldn't do shit on my own. I needed help, but a guy like me doesn't have a whole lot of options in that department. Luckily, I had one. I only hoped one would be enough.

Vikash was the new kid in seventh grade. Some days I was the only thing standing between him and another beating. Weird accent, funny name, strange bag lunches. Viks hit the trifecta of outcast nerd kid, but I always liked something about the little freak.

We kept in touch after high school when he did the normal thing Indian kids do: he went to a great university, graduated with honors and now works for the government in homeland security or something. High tech computer something or other. Smart shit. He's got a clearance level. I don't know what number, or even if I did I have no clue how high up the clearance ladder that would be, be he's got one.

Better than I got: A job at a now destroyed car rental company and a new job as drug recovery agent.

So I called Viks to ask a favor.

"Hey, man," he said. I know he didn't like me to call him at work, and truthfully we hadn't talked in a few months.

"Viks, what's up, dude?"

"Not much. How've you been?"

I looked out at the road, thought about what I was doing instead of sitting on my ass at the rental shop waiting for five o'clock. "Better. I've been better, I gotta be honest."

"What's up?"

"Well, I need to know if you can get on your little computer there and get me some information."

There was a pause on the line. I kept driving, headed toward Vikash's house, because I didn't know where else to go.

"You know I can't do that."

"It's nothing. One name I need to track by his credit card number. I really need to find this guy—"

"Brent. I can't."

His accent had almost completely vanished. Been a long time since the seventh grade. Reminding him of those days when I kept his briefs wedgie-free would have been met with more of this rules and regulations crap. I had to remind him that he owed me a serious favor.

"Viks, you owe me, man."

"I owe it to you to break the law? That's an abuse of the Patriot Act."

"Viks—"

"I can't just use the full resources of the federal government to help you find somebody."

"Vikash."

"And for what? Huh? Why do you need to find this guy so bad? Hire a private detective or something."

I let him run out of steam. Then, "Sandy would want you to."

More silence on the line and I knew my driving to his place was going to be worth the trip.

"Shit," he said.

"Yeah. Sorry, bro. That's the way it is."

I'd waited five years to cash in that chip. Five years since Sandy.

See, Vikash was never a ladies man. He's still about ninety-five pounds despite being six-foot one. He has buck teeth, too. And for some reason American girls don't think Indian guys are exotic the way American guys think the women are. Same goes for Japanese or Chinese. Asian girls can get attention from any guy in a bar, an Indian guy or a Chinese guy had better stick to his own kind. Not sure what that says about American girls, but it's been the truth of Vikash's life since I've known him.

So he's been known to partake of the occasional escort. Not street hookers. Professional ladies who are expensive, but earn it.

Sandy was one of those professional ladies.

Viks had taken her out on a few occasions. She'd been very nice to him. He'd taken her to fine dining establishments and she'd repaid in kind back at his place. But those visits didn't come cheap, and he ended up with quite a bill.

A bill he couldn't pay.

Sandy began harassing him for payment. She was good at it, too. She'd call, find him in public and embarrass him. She was relentless, even when he tried to give her a schedule of payment.

Finally he called me for help. I had to go deal with Sandy.

Maybe it was my dead-end job aspirations. Maybe it was that I'd protected him all those years in school. I don't know why he thought of me to go scare off his hooker-stalker. But it turned out I was quite good at the job. I fronted him some cash and paid her half of what she was demanding and made it known that their relationship was done. She was never to contact him again, and she didn't.

Earned me one favor, and there I was driving down the freeway, calling it in.

"What's the credit card number?" he said.

I smiled and read it to him off the receipt I'd pinched from the wreckage back at the rental shop. Sean Griffin, Visa card, expires August of 2018.

"Meet me at your place in an hour," I said.

"How about I get it to you tomorrow."

"No way. Gotta be today. ASAP. Just take an early lunch."

"I usually don't take a lunch."

"What do you mean you don't take lunch?"

"I eat at my desk. I don't like them to see me away from my work."

Different work ethic, that's for damn sure. I guess that's why a guy like Viks would never find himself in a situation like mine. Unless, of course, some asshole he used to know dragged him into it.

"Just be there, Viks. Sandy would want—"

"Fine. I'll be there."

He hung up on me.

22
SKEETER

If not a bump of something up my nose then at least a motherfucking Dr. Pepper or some shit. I was crawling out of my goddamn skin.

I decided to call in the update. Figures I couldn't get through to Corgan. Got some shitbag middle man punk.

"I'm on his ass now," I said. "No clue where's he's headed."

"You think he's got a line on our merchandise?"

"He sure as shit lit outta there like a rocket when the cops showed up. Must mean somethin', right?"

"Well, stay on him. Clyde left the hospital so maybe he knows something, too. Hopefully the asshole you're tailing is getting his orders from Clyde."

"You want I should go after Clyde instead? Isn't he the man in charge?"

"No. Stay on that one. We got ways to keep Clyde in line."

I figured I'd poke the dick weed with a stick a little bit. "Those are orders direct from Corgan?"

"Might as well be."

"What's that mean? You're the puppet and his hand is up your ass?"

I wasn't even sure which kiss-ass yes man I was talking to. Like frat boys and NBA fans, they all look the same to me.

"Just keep on following your guy, Delivery Boy. Call in again if anything happens."

He hung up, pissed off. Like I gave a shit.

So, fine. I follow this Brent guy for a while and hope he happens to drive right to where the Tahoe is. Sounds like a hell of a plan.

But goddamn, any drive is a better drive with a little speed in your veins. I knew it for a fact—first thing I was gonna do when this shit was done with, was get good and high for three days. I needed the damn vacation.

23
CLYDE

I managed to slip my jacket off before I fell into my car. My shirt was covered with dirt, blood, and sweat and I smelled like one of the homeless guys that asked for change downtown. I started the car, turned the air on high and then I pulled down the visor and checked myself in the rear-view. Shit. I looked like hell. Double shiners were already puffing themselves up from my bruised face, pushing my eyes toward my nose in what could have looked masculine if I hadn't looked so terrified.

For a crazy minute I felt like bolting, just starting the car and heading south, toward Florida and maybe Cuba from there. Let Madeline and the baby take their chances with Corgan. They were innocent, after all. Madeline was clueless about what I'd been up to. Plus, she had two sisters—one in Trenton and one in Boston. One of them would look after her and the baby.

It was a shitty thought. Shame warmed my face. Blood dripped from my nose onto my khakis and I fished around in the glove box for a Kleenex and found nothing but the stupid CD of whale sounds we kept in the car in anticipation of Madeline's labor. It had been in there for the last five months. We bought it and stored it for the big day and then I guess we never gave it another thought. I rested my head on the steering wheel and thought about my wife. I'd really fucked things up. She had to be wondering where I was. Had the fat nurse told her I'd been walked out by two thugs? Were the necktie twins back in there, threatening my family?

I needed to head east, that much I knew for sure. I just didn't know exactly where I needed to go. I needed to call Brent to figure it all out, but first I needed to talk to Madeline.

I pulled out of the hospital parking lot, struggling to see through swollen eyes, tasting blood, swallowing it, knowing it was dripping from my nose onto my shirt and my pants. My shirt was drying in the blast from the air conditioner and I shivered a little. They'd been careful not to break my phone. I dialed Madeline, swerving to miss an old lady in a crosswalk. Horns sounded and my tires squealed, but no harm no foul. The call went to voice mail. I listened to her voice tell me to leave a message. At the beep I took a breath. "Madeline. God. I don't know what to even say. I'm in my car. There's something I have to do. It's urgent or I wouldn't have left you. But listen to me. You have to stay safe. After the baby comes, don't let him or her out of your sight. That's important. Don't let the baby out of your sight. Stay together, no matter what that fat nurse says to you. Got it? I love you, babe. I love you so much. I'll be back as soon as I can."

She would be pissed, but she would forgive me. Maybe. Corgan said he'd give me half. Not as much as I'd hoped, but enough to set us up decently. And my kid would still have a dad, provided I didn't end up in jail.

The phone buzzed just as I hung up and the hospital's number flashed onto the screen.

"Madeline," I said, hating that my voice sounded choked.

"Sir, this is Starla Johnson. I'm one of the nurses at Richmond General. We've been trying to locate you in the building, sir, but you didn't answer any of the pages."

"I'm not in the building. Is Madeline okay?"

"Well, we figured you weren't in the building, that's why we called your cell phone. Just a minute, please."

What the fuck? Was Madeline okay? I needed to call Brent.

I merged onto I-64 East and joined the traffic moving at a snail's pace toward the historic triangle and Busch Gardens. Everyone was ready for some good, old-fashioned fun in the sun. The nurse's muffled voice rose and fell as she talked to someone else. Who? Another nurse? Madeline? "Hello?" I said. "Is Madeline okay?"

She came back on the line. "Madeline's fine, but there has been some trouble."

I thought of the men in the neckties. "Listen, those men are not relatives. Keep them away from my wife."

"I'm sorry, what? I'm not sure what you mean."

"Those men. The ones in the neckties. They aren't family. Keep them away from my wife."

She backed off again, yelling at someone to hurry up and get scrubbed, the surgeon was on the way. My stomach clenched and despite the cold blast of the A/C, sweat started to bead again on my smelly shirt. "Fuck, fuck, fuck," I breathed.

"Excuse me?"

"Sorry," I said. "What's going on? What's happening?"

"There's been a complication. Your wife is asking for you. We'll be taking her into surgery. I don't think at this point you'll be allowed in, but we'll be in O-R three in Maternity."

"Is she in danger?"

"We don't believe so, but—" and then she was gone again.

"Is she okay? Is the baby okay?"

"I'm sorry, Mr. McDowd. I have to scrub in. The surgeon is here. Come as soon as you can." She hung up.

"FUCK!"

The phone buzzed again. Brent. I picked up. "They're headed to Williamsburg," he said.

24
BRENT

I had to wait a half hour outside Viks's apartment building. When he finally showed up and let me into his place I got ready for the questions, but he kept quiet.

"Aren't you gonna ask?" I said.

"I don't want to know."

Fair enough. He seemed grumpy, but I guess I understood why. He tapped a few things on his laptop, accessed his computer at work or something and before I knew it his printer was humming with a rundown of every credit card transaction the Griffin family made starting from back in Detroit twenty-four hours ago on to ten minutes ago.

"Holy shit," I said. "You can really trace someone like this?"

Viks looked at me like I'd asked to see naked pictures of his mom. "Yes. You're not supposed to, but you can. I can get fired for showing you, but you can. We can both get arrested, but you can."

"Okay, let's not start that shit again."

"This is it, right, Brent? No more favors."

"Last and only one, I promise."

He handed me the single page, still warm from the printer. Not much on it. There was a fast food place back in Detroit, a charge from one of those magazine, gum and airsick pill shops in the Detroit airport terminal and one mini-mart charge here in Virginia that I guessed was traveling supplies like sodas and chips and whatever else a family that fat and Midwestern would keep in the car. Then a meal at a Waffle House.

Viks got on the internet and using the store number locations on the receipts, we could see where the places were where they stopped. It drew a semi-straight line toward the coast and Williamsburg, which meant either the Colonial history-buff shit or Busch Gardens.

Better than nothing.

"Thanks, Viks. This is awesome."

"Okay, I wanna know," he said.

I folded the paper and put it in my back pocket. "I don't think you do."

"I'm risking my job and jail time for this. I wanna know who the hell this guy is and why you need to find him so goddamn bad."

Like I said, Viks is not an intimidating specimen and this was about as heated as I'd ever seen him get.

"For your own good, Viks, you do not. Just know that it's not my doing. I'm looking as a favor for a friend. And this friend of mine, my boss really, he got me tangled up in this shit and so I had to get you in it and I'm super sorry, but the less you know the better."

"Am I in any danger?" Viks accent came out more when he was stressed. He was starting to sound like he was just off the boat.

"Fuck, no. Not a bit. With this info," I patted my hip pocket, "I'll have this taken care of tonight."

I went to the door, thinking I needed to call Clyde and give him the update.

"Thanks again, Viks. Seriously. This is a life saver." I hoped I didn't mean that literally. Flashes of the Tahoe coming through the window at my head came back to me. And the way Clyde had been talking, these guy were serious shit and they weren't keen to wait too long to get their merchandise back.

"I really hope I covered my tracks well enough on this," Viks said.

I hated to, but I left him to deal with that end of it on his own. I should have been more worried—it's not like he would take the fall for me. He'd sing like canary at the first sign of trouble and tell anyone who would listen that I'd strong-armed him into breaching national security, which I guess I did. Didn't take much arm twisting though.

Either way I'd end up in Guantanamo or something. So, great, life in prison as an enemy combatant or beheaded in the street by a drug cartel. Nice life choices I'd come to.

These guys Clyde was dealing with didn't exactly seem like cartel guys, not like I would know. But that Skeeter guy sure wasn't any criminal mastermind. He wasn't even Mexican.

Bug shit crazy for driving a Tahoe through my shop, but I couldn't tell yet if that put him in the ranks of a beheader.

I got back in my car and dialed up Clyde.

"They're headed to Williamsburg," I said by way of greeting.

"You found them?" The eagerness in his voice made it crack and squeak.

"Not yet, but we got them narrowed down to a reasonable area."

"Family of tourists," Clyde said, reasoning it out the same way I did. "One of two places."

"I can take Williamsburg first."

"I'll do Busch Gardens."

"Shouldn't you be with Madeline and the baby?"

Now the exasperation in his voice made it sink low. "There's been some trouble. She's going into surgery, and, dude, if we don't find that car really fucking soon, it's not going to make a bit of difference. My kid is never gonna see his dad at all."

25
SKEETER

I had two choices: follow the douche again like a homeless puppy dog looking for a bone, or go inside and talk to whoever the hell he just went to see.

Chances were real strong whoever was in that apartment knew where Brent was goin' anyhow, so inside I went. I'd seen the door he left from so I knew just where to go. I knocked and an Indian answered the door carrying a laptop bag and a heavy sweat on his forehead. And when I say Indian I don't mean like the guy on the Redskins helmet, but a real honest-to-Vishnu Indian fella.

He sure as shit didn't expect me, and I didn't want to disappoint.

I pushed him back inside his cracker box apartment.

"So what did my buddy Brent want with y'all?"

"What? Who are you?"

Funny accent and everything. Classic. "I said Brent's a buddy of mine, and I want to know what you two talked about."

"Are you the boss?"

I liked the sound of that. "Yeah, I'm the boss far as you're concerned. What did you tell him?"

He got all squinty eyed on me, like he was deciding how deep my bullshit was.

"I told him nothing."

"Wrong answer, Gandhi." I punched him in his stomach and I thought my hand would go straight through, the bastard was so goddamn skinny. He bent in half and dropped his bag. I never met a man before that didn't give one ounce of resistance.

"So tell me, what did you two chat about? Old girlfriends? Baseball scores? SUVs?"

"He had me look..."

The guy was so out of breath from my one shot that he couldn't even get a goddamn sentence out of his mouth. I felt so bad for the guy I had to motivate him a little further, so I stepped on his hand. I laid into it with the heel of my boot and felt the bones crunch around a little. I didn't break nothing, but I could have. Gotta start somewhere though so's you got leverage for later.

"Had you look for what?"

"Had me look up credit card receipts."

"What the fuck for?"

"Somebody. A guy. I don't know who."

He started crying like a girl. Now, I don't know if it was a good thing he didn't give anything back—because my nerves were a bit frayed and I don't know how well I'd do if I had to go up against anyone with too much to give—or if it sucked because I was so on edge that I just really wanted to kick the crap outta someone.

Either way the little pussy started pissing me off.

"Shut off the fuckin' waterworks and talk straight. Who did he want you to check on?"

"I tell you I don't know." His eyes were squeezed shut and he ground his teeth together. I don't know if he'd ever been in so much pain, and I hadn't even started yet.

I lifted my boot and he tucked his hand inside his other one and held it like a sick kitty. Just for that I kicked him the ribs. The toe of my boot could crack walnuts so a rib or two was a given thing if I kick a man in his cage.

"Well, where the fuck is he going to next?" I shouted.

"He's following the printout."

I kicked him again. "What printout?"

The Indian squirmed on the ground like a squashed bug. He was so long and lean it seemed like he was some kind of centipede.

"The one I gave him."

"Well, fuckin' give me one, too."

He had to get out his laptop and boot it up, which took a while because of his broken ribs and squished hand and all. I saw the screen and it had a bunch of lines like a bank statement or something. Payments for McDonald's and a Gas N Stop. The name on the account wasn't any Brent, it was some guy named Sean Griffin.

Now, I ain't a smart man, but I also ain't a dumb one. I'm looking for a missing SUV, Brent's looking for a missing SUV. He gets this list for some Griffin guy. Don't take more than my five grades to figure this is our man who has my car.

I snatched the paper off the printer tray as soon as it came out.

"This is what you gave him?" I said as I shoved it in the Indian's face.

"Yes. Just that sheet, that's all."

"You swear to God, or all the gods you believe in?"

"I swear on my life."

"Well, your life doesn't mean shit right now so you can do better than that." When I'd watched Brent leave he didn't have anything in his hand, so I was inclined to believe the little bastard. Then the printer spit out another page.

"I thought you said just that sheet?"

"It was. Only one page. I swear it." He started getting the doomed man's high pitch. His voice raised up a few octaves like he'd been kicked in the balls. He knew something bad was coming down if I thought he'd lied to me.

I grabbed the other page. It had a single listing on it from a Holiday Inn near Williamsburg.

"Is this where he's going?"

"I don't know. That transaction must have just gone through. I only gave Brent one page. Just one."

He still cradled his mashed up hand and he bent at a funny angle in the middle from the bad ribs. I felt like he was trying to lean away from me so I wouldn't hit him again. Hit him? I coulda kissed him. Brent didn't have this page, he said. I checked the time on the transaction. Four minutes ago. Mr. Griffin was in a Holiday Inn, and Brent didn't know it.

As a way of thanking the Indian for his help, I kicked over his chair. He'd almost leaned all the way out of it, so I only helped him over the edge. He went crashing down and bounced his head off a weird little low coffee table with a brass elephant on it.

I left him on the floor, crying again. I hoped Mr. Sean Griffin would be better company.

26
SEAN

We got a second floor room with a little balcony that overlooked the pool. Linda was still pouting because I snapped at her.

"I just wanted you to park closer to the door to let us get the bags out," she said. "You didn't need to bite my head off."

I don't know why I felt bad about it. Linda could find a way to be pissed about anything. Somewhere along the line she got it in her head that being a woman meant being angry and overworked and being married meant fighting all the time. It was bullshit really. And I'd been married to her long enough to call a bitch a bitch. And Linda was a bitch. But, she was still my wife. And in this particular instance, the mess we were in really wasn't her fault.

Chad and Becky changed into their suits and headed down to the pool. Linda called room service and ordered ice cream sundaes. She'd eat two of them and then be mad at me for letting her do it. Still, I refrained from pointing out it had only been an hour or so since we'd eaten and that she'd made me promise before we left Detroit not to let her eat too much during our trip. Christ, I wouldn't win. I couldn't win, no matter what I did.

She hadn't spoken to me since we checked in. She really hadn't spoken at all except to call room service. I could hear Chad and Becky down in the pool splashing around. I peeked out the window to make sure they were okay. Already they were turning pink in the sun. Linda was normally insistent about sunblock and sunglasses, but when she was in the a pout, she was a little more lax about things. This way, she could blame me for their sunburns.

"Hey," I called out the window. "Put this on." I tossed a bottle of Coppertone down to them and turned to face Linda.

"We've got to talk," I said.

She pursed her lips and flared her nostrils, but at least she looked at me. It looked like she was going to say something, but a knock on the door took her away. She disappeared down the tiny hallway to the door and came back leading a kid in a polyester getup that was supposed to look like a tuxedo into the room. He sat the tray on one of the beds and handed Linda the ticket to sign.

"Not me, son," she said, sitting down and picking up a dish of ice cream. "Give it to him." She gestured to me with a spoon. "He's Mr. Moneybags."

The kid cleared his throat and held out the ticket. I added a tip, signed it, and handed it back. When he left I sat next to Linda.

"I need to talk to you," I said.

She was still angry, still pouting. Her nostrils flared again as she took a bite of ice cream. She turned it over in her mouth. "So talk," she said.

I looked down at my hands as if staring at them would let me know what to say, would guide me through the next few minutes.

After a minute she put down the spoon. "Well, Jesus," she said. "Now you're starting to scare me."

I cleared my throat and looked at her. She had a little bit of chocolate syrup in the corner of her mouth. I wondered if I still loved her. Maybe this was what it was to be married, to sit beside someone you didn't really even like very much and tell them the bad shit you've done, knowing that they'll stick with you mainly because they have to.

It wasn't like I murdered anyone. I just took money that was rightfully mine. Somehow, I knew Linda wouldn't see it that way. And yet, she was it. She was all I had and someone at that car lot was trying to get in touch with me, had probably already called the police, and I just didn't know what else to do.

Throughout our marriage, it had always been Linda who had the answers, who ran the show. I earned the money, and she tucked it into our checking account and used it to make our little world run.

"What is it?" she asked. Her eyes narrowed and she licked at the little speck of chocolate on the corner of her mouth. "Oh my God, Sean. What did you do?"

I took her hands in mine, and I told her.

27
SKEETER

Holiday Inns, do they even have those anymore?

Another reason I really could use a new car was this thing didn't have a damn GPS. Why the hell should I poke around the darkness like a blind man who lost his cane when I can get maps from space beamed right to my dashboard? I tell you, what I couldn't do with a decent goddamn paycheck for once.

I thought out loud, "Corgan better damn well appreciate this when it's all over. Otherwise, next load I may just up and run off with myself. I ain't even met the man but I'll be good and goddamned if this Griffin dude thinks he's got more balls than me."

I spotted the hotel by the sign off the highway. A tall orange and blue lighted thing that might as well have been a big ol' ATM sign for me. Payday.

I pulled off and found my way to the parking lot and went way round back to park in the shadows. I took my keys with me and tried to decide if I was gonna move the shit from the Tahoe into my own car, or finally ditch the old rust bucket and take the Tahoe as originally intended.

Yeah, better to do that. Corgan hated it when the plan got altered.

Now, to find out what room our Mr. Griffin is in. The guy behind the counter wore a sweater vest so I immediately picked him out as a queer. Flirting with a fine young gal fit right in my wheelhouse, but I wasn't gonna get no information by acting like I wanted to suck this guy off behind the vending machines. Some things just ain't worth it.

I decided to go for confident with minor annoyance. Anyone in the service industry just wants to get you out of their face if they think you're going make their day even two percent more difficult.

"Hey, hoss. My uncle check in yet?"

I set my bare arms on the counter and started drumming my fingers. They hate that.

The queer boy made a face like someone had just cut a fart and asked, "And who is your uncle?"

"Griffin."

He typed a few things into the keyboard, but then turned and looked out to the pool.

"I believe the Griffins are on our pool deck."

I followed his look and saw two chubby kids getting set to do cannonballs in the pool outside. I didn't see any grownups and I didn't figure a pair of teenagers to steal my Tahoe and my load, but if Mom and Dad were out there on a lounge chair I'd just have to invite them inside where we could talk privately.

"Thanks, hoss," I said and let him get a good long look at my ass as I went.

28
SEAN

Linda stared at her feet, letting the sundaes melt in their dishes. "I don't know what to say, Sean. I don't know what to say." Her lips made that funny twitchy movement they do whenever she's mad.

Kids' voices floated up and into our room along with the smell of chlorine. It was the sort of sound that would have made me want an afternoon nap on any other day. I felt like I had been up for days, worrying about getting caught, waiting for it to happen.

"So what the hell are we supposed to do now?" she asked. "I suppose I should call my parents."

"No, Linda. Don't call them. If you call them it will just make things worse."

"Jesus, Sean, how could things get any worse? You're a criminal for God's sakes. A fucking loser criminal."

Someone down below in the pool did a cannonball and squeals erupted, followed by giggles. I hated to think of Linda calling her parents. We were already planning to visit them and that visit would go the same as all the others, with or without my criminal activities. Her mother would ask her, ever so slyly, why she hadn't married that nice Michael Turner with the big ears. Such a nice boy.

I had ignored her blathering for years, but lately, I had been wondering the same thing myself. Linda probably should have married Michael Turner with the big ears. Then she'd be his problem.

She was still talking, incessantly talking. I imagined wrapping my hands around her neck and squeezing the life from her pasty face.

A knock at the door interrupted her tirade.

I left her sitting on the bed beside the ice cream dishes and dirty napkins.

A skinny kid in a dirty, sleeveless T-shirt stood at the door.

"Give me your fuckin' keys," he said.

A lot of things ran through my head right then, like somebody was going to see this piece of trash asshole standing in the hall outside my door...like Linda was going to freak out when she saw him...like how the hell did he get all those tattoos on such scrawny arms...like what the hell had he been doing to get such rotten teeth? But the main thought that came in, the one that blocked out all the others and screamed at me in stereo, was that he'd been sent from Detroit to break my thumbs or cut off my dick, or arrest me. Maybe he was one of those Dog the Bounty Hunter types.

All those thoughts happened in rapid fire motion, one after the other and while I was just finishing up, he pulled back one of those scrawny little arms and landed a ringed fist right in my gut. I sank to my knees, my hand involuntarily reaching for the little shit. He backed up a step, kicked me to the side, and moved around me into the room. "I said give me your fuckin' keys."

"Ack, ack," came out of my mouth. I was trying to tell him to fuck off.

He moved down the tiny hall into the bedroom where Linda was. Good luck, Chuck. She was pissed off and had just eaten two ice cream sundaes. No way in hell was she going to put up with any shit.

"Who the hell are you?" I heard her say.

I crawled in their direction on all fours, sucking wind. When I was finally able to push myself to my feet, it was to the sight of the skinny dude holding a gun on Linda. "I need the keys to your car," he said.

"You look like the sort who could just hot wire it, so why don't you do that." Linda crossed her arms in front of her.

"We don't want any trouble," I said. "I'll give the money back."

"Jesus Christ, you moved the load? You liquidated it? It wasn't yours to sell, you FUCK!" He shot a hole in the floor.

For a second I was afraid the kids would hear the shot and come running, but the gun wasn't too loud. It sounded more like a firecracker and with the amount of noise everyone at the pool was making, it probably didn't even register as a sound to them.

"I'm on vacation," Linda said. "I've waited five years for this and I'm not going to have it ruined by some wiry little shit in a jean vest."

"Fucking cow," he said and pointed the gun at her.

I shot off the bed and aimed for his tiny little legs. I was about four times bigger than he was and I knocked him into the low dresser that held the TV. We fell to the floor with me on top. The gun flew out of his hand and landed somewhere by the sliding glass doors. Linda had hefted herself off the bed, grabbing the room service tray as she stood. The ice cream dishes flew, spraying the dingy carpet with chocolate syrup and strawberry sauce. She hefted me from the kid with one arm, tossing me aside like I was nothing but dirty laundry. It occurred to me to wonder how I had never noticed she was so strong, but then she brought the tray down on the top of his head with a loud TWANG! The kid's eyes fluttered once, twice, and then they closed.

"Did I kill the little shit?" she asked. "I hope I killed him."

"Jesus, Linda. We gotta get out of here."

"Is that one of the creeps you work with? Is this what I have to look forward to the rest of my vacation?" She was zipping suitcases and putting them by the door. "Move it," she said.

I grabbed as many as I could. A brisk sweat had started under my arms and around my neck. My gut ached where he punched me. It also hurt deeper. Maybe I was going to have a heart attack. Maybe I would just die. Who the hell was I married to?

We moved out through the hall, down the stairs and past the checkout desk. I had already paid with my credit card. They'd track me down. There was no question of that. They'd find the guy in our room, the bullet hole in the carpet, and I'd be in jail.

I stowed the bags in the Tahoe and climbed in. It had already cooled off a little when Linda showed up, towing two wet, sun-baked, pissed off teens behind her.

29
BRENT

Some lights are meant to lure you in, like a bug to one of those zapper things. Other lights make your gut seize up and make you want to turn and run the other way. Things like police lights.

There's something unnerving about cop lights on without the siren. The urgency is gone and that means something happened, as in past tense. As in, move along, nothing more to see here. An ordinary space, say a Holiday Inn, becomes a crime scene.

I drove by slowly, the elation I felt when I saw the sign off the highway oozing out of me like a nice buzz wearing off. When Viks had called me and told me about both the weird guy who came in and beat the crap out of him and the new credit card charge for Sean Griffin, I felt guilty that he'd been beaten, but thrilled that I had the new lead.

Of course I knew exactly who the guy was who terrorized Viks. Skeeter, the same jerk-off who crashed a Tahoe though a wall at my face. Had to be him. And he had a lead on me. I asked Viks how long it had been since Skeeter was at his house and he told me fifteen minutes. After I yelled at him for tending to his wounds first and not calling me immediately, he had to get off the phone since the ambulance had arrived to take him to the hospital to get his ribs set and his hand x-rayed... I felt bad all over again.

I hope I looked like any other rubbernecker as I drove by the scene. Three police cars, their lights in an unsynchronized frenzy of red and blue, crowded around the main entrance of the hotel. A guy in a sweater vest who I took to be the manager was speaking to a cop, waving his arms and describing the evening's activities in animated detail.

I almost drove over the curb when I saw Skeeter. He was sitting on the back bumper of a police car with an ice pack on his head and telling his version of events to a different cop. I was too far away to hear anything so I parked and got out to join the small crowd of onlookers.

I kept away from Skeeter and tried to stand close to the manager and get some of the story. The cop was taking notes.

"And then they just left?"

The manager swung his arms around and moved his fingers to indicated the quick shuffling of feet. "They all piled in their car and just took off. The kids still had bathing suits on." He waited for the cop to be as amazed as he was. The cop gave him nothing.

"Did you see what kind of car it was?"

"Chevy Tahoe. Black."

Shit. Our car. So the Griffins still had it. I didn't know yet if that was a good or a bad thing.

"License plate?" the cop asked.

"I didn't get the number, at least not all of it. It had a six." I breathed a small sigh of relief, but the guy in the sweater vest went on. "I did notice it had a license plate cover. Y'know those things that go around it and advertise, like, the dealership or something?"

"Yeah," the cop said, disinterested in any detail except the license for his report.

"Well, it was for a car rental place. Clyde McDowd Rentals. I remember it because it sounded so weird. Like, who rents from a cheap ass place like that?"

A cold chill broke out over my body. It would all be coming back to us. Damn it damn it damn it. I heard what I needed to. The SUV was gone, now the cops knew where it came from and apparently Skeeter hadn't been able to loosen it from Sean Griffin's grasp. What that last bit of information meant I wasn't sure, but I needed some advice, or at least to pass the cold sweats on to someone else.

I called Clyde.

"Forget it, they're on the run again," I said.

"What? How do you know?"

"I'm parked outside the hotel they registered at, but they're gone with the Tahoe and they left behind a crowd of cops and our pal Skeeter with a lump on his head."

"How the fuck did that happen?"

"I don't know and I'm not about to ask him or a cop for the story."

I debated telling him about the license plate cover, but I could hear the panic in his voice. The man was about to be a father, how could I shit on his happy day anymore? The news would keep.

"Look," I said, "you stay with Madeline. I'll keep after Griffin. At least we know we're close."

"What the fuck is Skeeter gonna tell Corgan?"

"We can't help that. As long as he gets his load back, he'll be fine." I didn't know what the hell I was talking about, but it made me a little calmer to hear it. Maybe it would do the same for Clyde.

"Alright. Shit. Call me as soon as you know something, okay?"

"Will do."

I drove away, leaving the silent flashing lights behind.

30
CLYDE

I pulled over to the side of the road and reminded myself to breathe. Purple Tie and Blue Tie could still be at the hospital. It was entirely probable that they were there watching over Madeline, waiting for my kid to be born. I gripped the steering wheel tight. Traffic shot past me, causing the car to shudder in a spasm of summer air. I thought of calling Madeline, of asking her to understand, but that would only make me look like a bigger asshole. This wasn't for her to understand. This was my mess and all I could do now was try to clean it up.

I pulled back out into traffic wondering if I should eat something. It was past lunchtime, coming on toward dinner. Would I still be alive at sunset? The thought turned my bowels to water.

I pulled off at the first exit, used the restroom, and got back on the highway heading west, toward Richmond. I drove ninety, planning to use the "my wife's having a kid" line as an excuse. It was the truth and I'd already exploited Madeline and the baby so what was a little more bullshit added to the steamy pile.

It was 4:30 by the time I got there and hot enough to buckle asphalt if the humidity got any worse. I got out of the car and immediately stepped in a piece of fucking gum. It was half liquid from the heat, and I dragged it in soggy pink strings across the parking lot and into the hospital with me. By the time I got to maternity, I had walked it all off and an orderly was swearing loudly somewhere behind me. "Goddamn gum."

Madeline was awake but groggy.

"Where have you been?" she'd been crying.

I sat on the bed and took her hand. "How is it going?"

"I just gave birth, you dick. You missed it." Fresh tears squeezed out from under her lashes.

The fat nurse ambled in. "I'm just about to go off my shift, Mrs. McDowd, but I wanted to give you something to help you sleep. You've had a long day. We'll wake you in a few hours and let you try to nurse her again." She glared at me as she jammed a needle into the port on Madeline's IV. "I see you managed to crawl back," she said.

"Work has been tough," was all I could manage to say. I was still focusing on the fact that Madeline had a baby. A girl. The nurse glared at me for a minute longer and then shuffled out.

Madeline pulled her hand away from me and turned to her side. "Go away," she said, but I ignored her. I sat beside her and waited until she was asleep.

When I emerged from the room, the heavyset nurse was gone and so was everyone else. I stopped an orderly, likely the one who had been swearing about the gum. "Where are the nurses?"

He looked around him like he was just noticing there was nobody at the nurses station. "It's five o'clock. End of shift. The new crew is probably making rounds."

I wandered to the nursery to see if I could catch a glimpse of my daughter. Venetian blinds had been lowered to cover the row of windows. I knocked softly, hoping to catch a nurse's attention. I could see movement beyond the glass, so I knocked a little harder. A blind lifted and a nurse in pink scrubs looked out. I held up my arm to show her I had a wrist band. Obviously a father, obviously I wanted to see my kid. She looked behind her and as she did, the shade moved enough to let me see that there were cops in the nursery with her. I backed up a step, feeling my heart drop to my shoes.

In my pocket, my phone buzzed. I pulled it out, already knowing what it was. A text message. I opened it. It was a picture of Purple Tie holding my baby.

31
SKEETER

Fuckin' cops. I was the goddamn victim! Yet there they were asking me all kinds of questions like who hit me and how did I end up in that room.

I answered everything right down the line. I said he was my uncle and I hadn't seen him for a while. I didn't realize there was still bad blood from a family incident I'd rather not discuss. They bought it. I'd lost my gun so they couldn't bust me for that. I knew all too damn well I didn't have the load of drugs on me, so I was clean in that regard.

What could they do but release me on my own recognizance? They even let me keep the ice pack.

I walked away thinking what I was gonna do when I saw the fat bitch again. And then the worse things I'd do to his wife. I thought I was walking up to ordinary joe citizen when I got the room number from those chunky kids. They were all too eager to give it up, too. Didn't even have to ply them with candy.

Then I walk in and she goes all Chuck Norris on me with a plate or some shit. We'll have our day, me an' her.

The car would have to stay. If I got in and drove off some cop would call in the plate number because he's a cop and they like to bust my balls, and that can only lead to trouble. I ended up walking about a half mile down the road and found a big ass Walgreen's with a half full parking lot.

I went inside and stuffed a flat head screwdriver down my pants, paid for a Red Bull and went to the farthest corner of the parking lot. I downed the drink and found a hunk of chipped-off brick I used to smash the window of a four door Buick. Probably some old person inside picking up a prescription. Though old people usually park close to the front since they can't walk great and shit. Well, whoever's car it was, the thing was about to be mine.

With my new screwdriver I had that thing up and running in

two minutes flat. Nothing to it when you got the skills I got.

The cops left me my phone since I wasn't a suspect or nothing. Don't leave town they said, but they always say that and I always say, yes, sir, even though I mean eat shit. I dialed up a guy I know who knows a guy I wanted to talk to.

"I need a number," I said. Time to get real about this shit. Red Bull ain't cuttin' it.

32
SEAN

My head pulsed. Linda was quiet, which was both good and bad. Chad and Becky were quiet, too. They were slightly sunburned and placid from their time at the pool, but that didn't stop them from being pissed about getting dragged away from the hotel after checking in just a few hours before. It was 6:00 so I pulled off the road and hit a drive-thru. Linda ate but was still quiet. It wasn't until we were halfway to Virginia Beach that she figured out where we were headed. "Seriously?" she said. "What the hell are we supposed to say to them?"

"Chad and Becky need a safe place to stay. You and I need to figure out what to do."

"I think it's obvious what you need to do, Sean. Turn yourself in."

"Turn yourself in for what?" Becky asked through a mouthful of fries.

"Nothing," I said.

"Did you do something wrong, Dad?" Chad asked.

I didn't answer. There was nothing I could say that would make any of this any easier. I was looking at doing time. If that guy back at the hotel was a bounty hunter I was screwed. Could I be accused of resisting arrest? Did that count when it was a bounty hunter? Christ, I was a fugitive.

We got to Ernie and Betty's house as dusk was settling in and the cicadas had come out in full chorus. It made my headache worse. Linda gave them hugs and sent the kids upstairs with the bags.

Betty gave me a tight-lipped look like she'd just swallowed a fly or smelled a fart. I managed a weak smile. Ernie stuffed his hands in his pockets and rocked back and forth on his toes. He used his pockets as a way to let me know he'd never shake my hand. He rocked on his toes to emphasize the fact that he stood a good five inches taller than me and that at age sixty-eight, he was still in top shape, like the marine he once was. Semper Fi, motherfucker.

I nodded and wished for a sandwich. Or a beer. Or death. Death wouldn't be so bad.

"We need to leave the kids here for a little bit," Linda said, surprising me by taking my hand. "Sean and I have some things to do."

"Oh, God," Betty said, "does this involve sex?"

Linda rolled her eyes. "We'll be back later."

"I hope it doesn't involve sex. Your children are at a very impressionable age."

We closed the door on Betty's still-nagging voice and climbed back in the Tahoe. I pulled out my phone to dial my brother's number. "What are you doing?" Linda asked.

"Turning myself in. I don't want another crazy guy showing up like that. He had a gun. Jesus, Linda."

"Just wait on that," she said. "Let's go grab a drink someplace. I need to think. We need to ditch this car. It's probably how that loser found us. He's probably been tracking my credit card."

"Where do we ditch it? And I'm not so sure that's a good idea. They have my name. If I just abandon it I'm liable."

She blew out a breath. "Remove the distributor cap. Pull off the hubcaps and the tires. Call it in like it's been vandalized."

I pulled into a gas station, not sure I wanted to add vandalism to the list of charges that were sure to be brought against me. Linda stayed in the car while I filled the tank part way and went inside to get some road snacks. I still had no idea what we should do, but I knew there was no way in hell I could do it without food. And the Arby's we'd eaten a few hours ago was no longer there to keep me satisfied.

When I got back to the car, Linda was pulling at a seam on the ceiling. "Is that part of your master plan to make it look like the car was chopped for parts?" I tore open a stick of beef jerky and started chewing.

"This seam is funny," she said, "like it was re-done. Maybe we can get them on giving us a car that was involved in a wreck or something."

"What would be the point in that?"

She looked at me the same way her mother had a few hours before. "To sue them, Sean. Because if we don't get some cash coming in to help pay for your defense after your brother gets done with you..." She went back to work on the seam.

"Shut the fuck up, Linda."

She got that look on her face she gets when she is about to start yelling at me. She opened her mouth to speak at the same time she had worked the thread from the seam loose.

A half dozen wrapped packets the size of flattened bricks dropped into her lap.

33
BRENT

The phone's vibrations startled me out of a deep thinking session, a session that came to the usual blank page my brainstorming resulted in. I welcomed the distraction from plotting the salvation of my ruined life, hoping it was Clyde with some news. I checked the caller I.D. and saw the number for the rental counter. Who in the hell could be calling me from the shop? Cops? Feds?

I pushed the phone away like it had sprouted fangs then I remembered I'd rerouted the calls coming into the shop to my cell phone like a good little employee. Clyde didn't deserve me, that was for damn sure.

"Hello, Clyde McDowd Rentals."

There was a too-long pause on the other end. "Um, hello?"

"Yes. I'm sorry I'm not in the office right now but if there's some issue with a vehicle—"

"Is this the guy I talked to this morning?"

How the hell should I know? Still, there was something familiar in the voice. "I was there this morning, yes. Who is this please?"

Another pause. This guy had something to hide. "Uh, Griffin. Sean Griffin."

I think I gasped out loud like an idiot. I know I nearly dropped the phone. "Holy shit. Mr. Griffin, where are you?"

"In Virginia." No shit, Sherlock. "Listen, I need to know if you're...um...missing something."

My excitement went cold. What the hell did that mean, missing something? Aw, who the fuck am I kidding, I knew what it meant. I needed to play it cool.

"We sure are missing that Tahoe of yours. I've been trying to get in touch so we could get it back."

"Are you missing..." His voice turned leering like a sex offender luring a little girl to his van. "Anything else?"

A woman's voice broke through the background and I thought I heard, "What the hell are you doing?" before his hand palmed over the phone and everything went muffled.

"Mr. Griffin? Mr. Griffin? Are you there?"

"Yes, I'm here." He was back and little bit breathless.

"Mr. Griffin, all I want is the car back." If he knew what was up, might as well lay it out there. "And all its contents. It's very important that I get it back as soon as possible."

"And you'll...pay?"

More protests from the woman I assumed was the fat Mrs. Griffin. I wondered if the kids were in on it, too. With my luck the little brats would be in the backseat snorting up the load and getting higher than a night of ice cream and cotton candy.

"Yes. We'll pay. Where can we meet?"

More phone-covering discussions were had before he came back on the line. "Tomorrow morning. Eight a.m. Virginia Beach."

"Tomorrow morning's too late. Can't we do it tonight?"

"Don't you need time to raise the cash?"

Fucking idiot. I had no intention of paying this asshole, even less so the longer he dragged this out. If I knew where and when he was going to be somewhere, this became someone else's mess to clean up.

"I just really need that car back, Sean." I pulled the name out of thin air. Guess more details of this wild day had been burned into my brain than I thought.

"Tomorrow morning."

It was better than nothing. "Yeah, yeah. Eight a.m. Give me the address."

As he told me where to meet my mind spun to my next call to Clyde and then his call to Mr. Big. Probably I was sending Griffin to his death by telling them where to find him, but he was currently digging his own grave on the other end of the line by making demands and striking deals he had no right to make to give back the load of drugs in the ceiling. He was only lucky he was talking to me. I'm a nice guy. These dudes Clyde was mixed up with wouldn't be so patient.

"I'll see you there. And Griffin, you better be there and you better have everything." My attempt at intimidation came out as more of a plea. Either way, he said he would. "And leave the kids at home."

Aw, crap. They were on vacation. Okay, at the hotel or with Aunt Zelda or whoever the hell there were here to see. So it wasn't the best ending to my first drug deal set up, but I finally had news to call Clyde about.

34
SEAN

Linda's mouth hung open. "Who are you? I don't even know you anymore." We were parked in a rest area north of Virginia Beach. The sun was setting, giving everything inside the car a weird, red glow.

One of the packets, cocaine I thought it was, slipped to the floor. Linda ignored it and kept her eyes on me. I tried to meet her glare, but I was thinking ahead, to our future.

"We could leave Detroit, Linda. We could go south, to Florida, start over. The kids' college would be paid for. I could leave the company, maybe even start my own."

She shook her head and shoved the rest of the packages onto the floor. Then she opened her door and climbed out. She took off walking in the opposite direction of the restrooms. I sat for a minute and then climbed out too. It was probably stupid walking away from a car loaded with drugs, but I needed her on my side if we were to pull this off. I followed her and caught her at the head of a narrow trail, just past a sign that read CLEAN UP ALL ANIMAL WASTE. There was dog shit everywhere.

She ducked under the cover of trees and I followed, wanting to call after her, but I was too winded and I was trying to avoid stepping in crap.

The nice thing about Linda is that she's just as fat and out of shape as I am. She stopped when the trail turned uphill. When I caught up to her I started explaining myself.

"I think we could pull this off, Linda. I think we could really do it. We could move, like I said. Just think about it."

It was dark under the trees and mosquitoes buzzed around my head. She put her hand on my forearm. "Shut up, Sean." She stepped closer, wrapped her arms around my neck. Then, pressing the bulk of her stomach against mine, she kissed me. I kissed her back, wrapping my fist in her hair. She smelled like sweat and donuts and Diet Dr. Pepper. We hadn't kissed in a while, and it had been even longer since we made love. Plus it was really hot and we were both sweaty. Still, we managed well enough. The clothes came off and we ended up on the ground in a small area with no dog poop. When we were done, Linda stretched out beside me and rested her head on her hand. The drone of trucks was hypnotic and I wished we could doze for a little bit. But the Tahoe was still up the trail and still filled with coke. Her breasts pressed against me. She always had great tits. I turned and kissed her. "We should get back to the car." She nodded and we fumbled in the dirt for our clothes, both scratching at the mosquito bites that covered us. We picked up some sodas and chips from the vending machines in the rest area shelter and climbed back in the car.

"Well, what now?" she asked.

35
CLYDE

Our daughter was missing. She didn't even have a name yet. Madeline and I hadn't been able to agree on names, so our child was just "Baby Girl McDowd." Madeline was sedated, but not enough to be oblivious to everything. She drifted to sleep, her eyes fluttering closed, only to snap open again after a minute, clutching my arm. "Where is she? Clyde, find her. Find her!"

The police had been called and then the FBI. The maternity ward was filled with guys in suits and uniforms, all of them asking questions and scribbling in their tiny notebooks. They all wanted to know about my black eyes, what happened to my face and clothes. I told them I was mugged, and then there were more questions about why I didn't file a police report. I must have answered the same question fifty different times. And how the hell does one describe a newborn? Tiny? Pink? Wearing a diaper and wrapped in a blanket?

My God, I hadn't even set eyes on her yet.

When they finally let me go, I sat and held Madeline's hand for a long time. She didn't ask me about my face. She looked at me with fear for our daughter and disgust, whether for my face or for the fact that I was the guy she was stuck with, I have no idea. Finally, she drifted off and stayed asleep, so I meandered the hallways and finally ended up in the waiting room. Cops were everywhere, talking to nurses, interns, orderlies. There was no way to slip out without drawing suspicion. I was itching to call Brent to see how he was getting along, to check on things. I wanted to call the assholes who had my daughter, but I deleted the picture they sent me out of fear that the cops would ask to see my phone. Maybe I was moving from scared to paranoid.

Then I thought of my baby again and tasted bile in the back of my throat. I was moving past fear to rage, thinking of the ways I'd waste Purple Tie and Blue Tie. Then I thought of how I'd track their boss down and waste him too.

I slipped into the bathroom and punched in Brent's number. "Tell me something good," I said. "They took the baby."

"Jesus fucking Christ," Brent said. "I'm so sorry. Man... that's...man, I'm sorry."

My eyes stung. I swallowed hard. "Did you find them?"

"Actually...they found me."

"What?"

He told me about the drop in the morning. Virginia Beach. "So I'll be there," he said.

"Me, too."

I pocketed my phone and slapped some water on my face. Back in the waiting room, I took a seat and watched, getting the lay of the land, checking exits and entrances, trying to memorize faces and figure out who was cop and who was FBI. My head pounded.

"Mr. McDowd?"

I shifted in the orange vinyl chair. The waiting room smelled of rubber soled shoes and old coffee. "Yeah?" I tried to look up at him, but the florescent lights shone right in my eyes, so I rested my elbows on my knees and stared at the floor, waiting for the next round of questions. His shoes were cleaner than mine, polished to shiny black mirrors.

"I need to ask you a few questions."

"Sure." I wanted to tell him to fuck off, but under the circumstances...

I wanted to slip out, track down the Tahoe, track down the necktie twins and make them dead. Then the goddamn fucking FBI could ask me all the fucking goddamn questions they wanted.

"Follow me, please." His shiny shoes turned the opposite direction, so I reluctantly pushed myself up and followed. He was shorter than me, but not by much. The suit he wore was expensive, but all wrinkled up in the back, like he'd been wearing it for a few days. I followed him through the maternity ward and out the secure double door with the security pad that was supposed to keep babies from being abducted.

He led me into an empty room. Once inside, he turned to face me. The room had been set up as some sort of makeshift office for him. He tossed his jacket on a small loveseat, his name tag face up. His name was Special Agent Stu Trumble. His briefcase lay wide open on one of the reclining wing chairs. Papers spilled out. "Is all that to find my kid?" I asked.

He shook his head. "Nah. Just PDFs of similar cases. I hate reading on computer screens so I asked my assistant to print them out." He looked around and shuffled his feet a little bit. "So anyway, you can sleep in here. I know you must be tired. We'll keep looking for your kid. I've found a lot of kids, you know. Been doing this a long time."

I asked him if he had kids of his own because I felt like it was something I should ask, something that would make me seem like I was just a dad looking for his daughter and not a cut-rate mule who made the mistake of trusting his assistant to do something right.

"I have four kids. Three boys and a little girl." He was younger than me by at least five years. His face was pink where he had shaved it earlier in the day and now, at eight p.m. was just starting to show a hint of five-o'clock shadow.

"Four kids," I said.

He smiled and patted me on the shoulder. "Get some rest. We'll come and get you if anything changes."

"Actually," I said, my mind waking up and starting to work again finally. "I'd like to take a shower, too, if that would be okay. Do you think they would let me borrow some scrubs or something?"

He jerked a thumb behind him, pointing to a tall armoire. "Delivery room, remember? All the scrubs for the dads are in there. Soap and shampoo in the bathroom." He smiled again and held up his fingers. "Four kids." Then he was gone and for the first time in a few hours, I was completely alone.

I hurriedly changed into scrubs, grabbed the I.D. tag from his jacket and opened the door. The nurses' station was to my left and was busy with cops, nursing staff, ringing phones. To my right was a stairwell. I took a deep breath and slipped out, hoping I was doing the right thing.

36
SKEETER

I can't believe I waited until I pulled over for my second bump. The first snort I'd done as soon as I handed over the money for the two bags of crystal. Couldn't wait no longer to charge the ol' batteries.

Out on an unlit two-lane the first bump started wearing off already. Fuckin' crap meth cut to shit with baby powder and corn starch. I laid out a line running up the length of my index finger and held it to my nose. I skronked it up with a mighty snot-clearing honk. Tiny sparkles hit the back of my eyelids and the gentle drip started down the back of my throat.

Now I could be up all night and figure this shit out. Whoo! No rest for the wicked. I drummed a Slayer riff on the steering wheel and tried to think of my next move. The Griffins were AWOL, the cops on the scent and the car rental dudes had about as much info on Griffin as I did right then.

Shit. Not a whole lot to go on. This was the kind of time when I wished I knew someone on the police force. I could call in the favor and have him look up license plates or credit cards or some shit. Maybe I needed to go visit that little Indian fuck again, get him to tappity-tap-tap on his computer and come up with another link to Griffin.

But, man, it would be so much easier to just call up a cop and find out what they know from the hotel and where they think the Tahoe went.

As if my prayers had been heard by Jesus H. his own self, a pair of headlights and two berries—one cherry and one blue—lit up my rear-view. Dammit.

I pushed down my packet of crystal into my shirt pocket and wiped my nose with my hand, checking my eyes in the mirror. Bloodshot, but averagely so. I prepped for Johnny Law to come around to the car, but this good ol' boy was taking his sweet mother-humping time. By the time he got to knockin' on my window I bet he'd gotten a year closer to retirement.

I powered down the window and he looked past me to the passenger seat with its broken glass and gaping hole where the passenger window was before I busted it out.

"Help you, Officer?"

"Why you stopped out here, boy?"

Oh, shit. We had ourselves a cracker. A real southern po-lice man. Woulda fit right in on screen in Smokey and the Bandit.

"Jus' makin' a phone call, sir. You know it's not safe to talk and drive." I smiled at him but his mirrored shades gave me zilch in return.

He leaned back and eye fucked the backseat, looked around at the trees on the side of the lane. We were alone. No accomplices. "Son, I had a report of this very car here being stolen this afternoon. You know anything about that?"

The crystal buzzed my brain and the seconds ticked by in double time until I answered him.

"No, sir. Could be my grandma didn't know I took the car today. She's gettin' a might forgetful what with the Alzheimer's and all that shit, y'know?"

He nodded slow. "Grandma, huh?"

"Yessir. I live with her so I can be there to take of her needs. She can still cook so it ain't all bad." I smiled and got nothing but my own gap-toothed reflection in his sunglasses.

"Son, step out of the car. And bring your license and registration with you."

"Well, like I say, the car's registered to my grandma you see—"

"Still want you to step out of the vehicle."

"Oh, sure, sure."

Dumb move, pig. That good ol' boy just signed his death certificate. I kinda wanted to ask him to see his license and ask to check his time of death.

He stepped back from my door and gave a look back to his patrol car. I looked too but I knew I wouldn't see another cop waiting in the car. If there were two of them, they woulda flanked me. The dumb ass was alone.

I shut the door behind me and shot my hand forward and had it on the butt of his gun before he turned his head back from his own car. He put a meaty paw over top of my hand, but I had momentum on my side. I yanked his revolver free and only had to move it six inches to the left and I was pointing it at his belly.

Kevlar vests hadn't reached the sticks yet. He wasn't no city cop used to being shot at. Besides, most of these Bible thumping NRA types thought bullet proof vests were for pussies. I put three shots in his stomach and while he was digesting those I lifted the gun and put one in his forehead. He went down and his shades never came off his face.

I went over to the cop car to stock up on whatever he was selling. There was a clipboard of bullshit paperwork, an extra set of cuffs, a cold half cup of coffee. I zeroed in on the shotgun clipped to a rack between the seats. I tugged on it, felt it move a tiny bit in the rack. I thought if I could just get it rattling around in there I could snap it out and have some serious firepower. I yanked and pulled and jerked and tugged, but that thing was more stubborn than a whore telling you to put on a rubber.

I tried like hell to get a better grip on the damn thing and wouldn't you know it, I shot a hole in the damn roof. My finger slid onto the trigger and blammo! The lights fizzled off on the blue side and the shot was louder than hell inside the car. I almost fell backward as I backed out to get away from the loud-as-fuck of it all. That was, like, Motorhead loud.

I decided to fuck it and leave the shotgun there. I did take the cop's badge and his radio. You never know when that shit could come in handy.

37
CLYDE

I made my way down the stairs and into the parking lot. Realistically it would have been better if I had a different car, but I didn't want to add that to the list of felonies I was committing. Besides, good ol' Special Agent Stu Trumble had told me to get some sleep, so he wouldn't be bothering me for several hours, unless something happened with Madeline. And she was a tough bird. Mostly I just had to worry about her popping her stitches when she kicked my ass. A couple of nurses heading in from a cigarette break nodded at me. I guess I looked pretty official in the scrubs. I nodded back and kept moving.

When I got into the car I dialed Corgan's number and waited for him to pick up.

"Clyde, my boy, good to hear from you."

"Don't hurt my daughter," I said, hating how desperate I sounded. "Jesus Christ, just don't hurt her."

"Calm down, Clyde," he said, chuckling like we were talking about a golf game or some run of the mill shit like that. "No one is going to hurt anyone. You've confessed your sin. All will be forgiven once you make it right."

"It was just a big misunderstanding, Mr. Corgan," I said.

"I know, son. I know."

"The car. My wife. She was in labor. The car wasn't in the usual place...my assistant..."

"Shhh. Shhh. Shhh. Now this isn't going to get us anywhere. What's done is done. Let's work together to make this right."

His calmness was terrifying. Sweat was soaking through the armpits of my scrubs. "The people with the Tahoe have contacted us."

"Well, that's good news," he said, sounding almost paternal. Hey, Dad, I just got an A in Geometry. "I knew you could do it if you just had the proper motivation."

I rested my head on the steering wheel, fighting tears. Please don't hurt my baby. "Yessir."

"Now tell me what they said."

"They know about what's in the ceiling."

"Ah. I see."

"They are meeting me tomorrow in Virginia Beach. I'll get the car back then."

"And the rest of my property, I assume."

"Yessir. Of course."

He sighed. "I'd like to believe you'd do it for the sake of our history together, Clyde. But I feel like perhaps you need to keep that feeling of motivation at peak level."

My heart pounded. "Sir?"

"Your daughter wants to talk to you."

"Oh God. No. Please, don't!"

I heard the sound of a tiny baby, breathing through the phone, making tiny grunting noises. She whimpered first, and then began to wail and cry. I climbed out of the car and paced, the phone clutched in my hand. I'm sure I looked like a crazy person, but it was night and there was no one around. I wanted it to stop. I wanted the noise to stop. I didn't dare hang up. I needed to tough it out with my baby. I needed to fix this for her.

"My goodness she can yell. Reminds me of my granddaughter." The crying stopped, faded, like someone was carrying her away.

"Don't hurt her," I said, my voice thick with tears.

"I trust you are motivated now."

"Yes. I'm motivated." I imagined myself shooting the fat fuck in the face.

"I know it is distressing to hear a baby cry," he said. "But in your case, I would recommend you be relieved when you hear her cry. You should worry when you no longer hear that noise."

"I'll get the stuff tomorrow." My jaw ached from clenching my teeth so tightly.

"I think I'll send one of my own men just to make sure things go as they should."

As far as I could tell, he already had three men on the job, Skeeter, the usual driver, and Purple and Blue Tie. There was nothing else I could say about that, so I said the only thing I could think of. "Please don't hurt my little girl."

"See you soon, Clyde." The phone beeped in my ear as he hung up.

38
SKEETER

All I have to say about that don't drive and talk on a cell phone crap? Fuck you, this is America.

So I answered the call when I saw it was Corgan. He told me about the meet scheduled for the morning. A pretty little package dropped right in my lap.

"So, what, you want me to get the dope and come on back? Or you want me to make them realize what a mistake they all made?"

I think Corgan sighed at me. "You'll be outnumbered."

"So?" I said. "I'll put them down first thing. No talking, no arguing, just bam, bam, bam. They all go down for what they tried to pull."

"Let me guess, that would raise your fee?"

I didn't like his tone, but he had called me out. I saw another way, though. "Not necessarily. If I do this job for you, maybe you think about moving me up a bit in the organization. I think I've proven myself over the years and now that I'm about to wrap up this cluster fuck—"

"But you didn't find them. Clyde did. He called me, not you."

"Well, sure. But I got right up their ass. Spooked them out of the bushes and now I'll go finish it. I think it shows I'm ready for the next step."

"We'll see."

Then the bastard hung up on me. It was an opening, at least. Not much of one, but I figured he wasn't in the mood to deal until this was all wrapped up, which would be the next morning.

I banged another bump of crystal up my nose and drove off to find a place to sleep. Damn, I sure ain't a morning person.

39
SEAN

Ernie and Betty were ambling around in the kitchen. I didn't hear the kids, which wasn't surprising. They were likely asleep. Linda and I had slept in a guest room off the family room in the back of the house. It had a tiny double bed that we crushed ourselves into and had the smell of old people...dust and mildew and just...oldness. I sat on the edge of the bed and listened to Linda breathe. I smiled a little, thinking of last night. Forty years old and still able to give my wife the high hard one.

I carried my clothes into the bathroom, showered, and got dressed. I had two days' worth of beard growing in and I'd be lying if I said I didn't look damn good. Linda had packed my suitcase for me, so I was stuck with putting on a pair of Bermuda shorts with palm trees and tiny martini glasses splattered all over them and a World's Best Dad T-shirt. I brushed my teeth and then I ripped the sleeves off the T-shirt.

Betty grunted as I poured myself a cup of coffee. "New shirt, Sean?"

I gave her a tight smile. "I'm on vacation."

Ernie had his face buried behind the newspaper. Every few seconds his hand snuck out from behind its folds and grabbed his mug of coffee. I didn't even bother to sit down. I stood at the sink and powered down the coffee. I'd get a Danish or something on the road. "I've got something to do this morning," I announced. "I'll be back later."

Betty sniffed like I'd farted after a plate of nachos and looked out the window above the sink. I headed for the door and remembered I'd left the keys in the bedroom. Shit and fuck. The last thing I needed was Linda tagging along. Bad enough that she was, well, a bitch. But on the serious side, what if something happened to me? What if I got shot or got in a wreck? Chad and Becky would need someone.

My flip flops slapped against the bottoms of my feet as I

tried to tiptoe through the family room to the guest room. I kicked them off. I picked up my jeans from the night before and fished around in the pocket. I grabbed them and turned to leave the room.

"Don't even think about it, Sean." Linda glared at me from the bed. Maybe it was more of a scowl. There was none of the "morning after" glow on her. She just looked bitchy.

"Don't even think about what?"

"Leaving without me."

"I want you to stay here. In case something happens to me."

She laughed a little bit as she tossed the blankets aside and stood. "Bullshit. I'm not staying here. Nothing's going to happen to you except that maybe you'll leave us all and go on your merry way."

She was working to get her boobs stuffed into her bra, taking her frustration out on them.

"I'm not going to leave you, Linda. I would never leave you and the kids."

She snorted. Seemed like there was a whole lot of that sound going on this morning. "Right. Whatever." She worked her feet into a pair of sandals and pointed to the bedroom door. "Let's go."

I couldn't help but notice she didn't brush her teeth.

40
BRENT

With the heater on the windshield fogged up in the morning chill. I tried to find the right balance. Heater on, window cracked. Defogger on, temperature up to eighty. It kept me occupied, at least. Gave me something to do. My fingers bounced from the heat controls to the radio in a futile search for something not coated in sugar and sung by a teenage girl.

I went on a mini rant in my head about the sorry state of music today. I watched the parking lot, the walking path along the beach side. Nobody. A few minutes earlier a guy had jogged past, but I knew damn well that fat bastard Griffin wouldn't be jogging.

I had no clue how this would all go down. I came to a drug deal with no money except for the twelve bucks in my pocket. Griffin was expecting money in exchange for the load. The dumb-ass never specified how much he expected to get, but I assumed it was north of twelve dollars. I guess his not asking for an amount was further evidence that neither one of us had any experience at buying and selling kilos of cocaine.

I checked the clock again. Still a half hour before the meet. I hadn't been able to sleep so I drove here to wait it out and fight with the condensation. I shouldn't have let myself get so distracted with other shit. I needed a plan and a way to get away from this clean. I had nothing.

A car pulled into the parking lot and I recognized it as Clyde's. He must have sped here. I didn't know if I should expect to see his wife and newborn in the back seat, but he was alone.

I tapped on the horn once and waved when he looked over. He got out and came to me, oddly wearing hospital scrubs. When he got in the passenger side he let in a gust of cold air and the equilibrium of my fog bank was thrown off.

He looked like a hangover had died on his face. Red veined

eyes, pale cheeks, bits of food stuck in his teeth. As rough as the past day had been on me, Clyde looked like he'd taken the brunt of it.

"Hey, man," I said. I figured not pointing out how bad he looked was a good move on my part.

"Hey," he said. "Nothing yet?"

"We got time still."

"What's the plan?"

"You didn't bring one?"

Clyde looked at me with a crooked face. "You have no plan?"

"I told him we'd pay him, but you know I can't do that."

"Well, I'm not gonna pay him."

"So he's not getting paid, I guess."

Clyde turned to face forward, his heavy breathing fogging the glass again in spots as the air blew hard to fight it. "We need to get those packages back."

"I know we do. And you can say drugs. We all know what the hell is in them."

"If we all know it, why do we need to say it?"

I nodded my head in silence. So that's how it was going to be. I risk my life to set things right on a deal that had nothing to do with me and he's going to go get all bitchy with me.

Then, like he read my thoughts, Clyde apologized. "Shit, I'm sorry, Brent. I'm fucking exhausted and my wife thinks I'm a deadbeat dad already. The kid's only been out for a day and already I'm the worst dad ever. This is just not what I needed right now."

"I know, man. It's cool."

We looked at each other and smiled. No bro hugs for us, a cheesy grin would have to do. Clyde's cell phone rang with a snippet of a Cat Stevens song, one I knew was Madeline's favorite. Clyde didn't even have to check the caller I.D. "Shit."

He clicked the phone on and held up a finger to silence me. "Hey, baby?"

Her voice was so loud and shrill, I heard every word in the confines of the car.

"Where the hell are you?"

"I had to take care of something. I'll be back real soon."

"Clyde? Clyde?" It was like she expected him to know the rest, and I think he did. He knew how completely ridiculous it was for him to take off at a moment like that. "Clyde, our daughter."

"I know, baby. I know. That's what I'm taking care of. If you just give me a little bit of time, she'll come back to us. I swear it. I promise."

"Clyde, what the hell did you do?"

"I promise, baby. Just a little while longer. I'll see you soon."

He was almost in tears as he rushed her off the phone. He had to hang up on her yelling, but he avoided the questions she hurled at him.

I didn't know what to say to him. So I just said, "I'm sure it will be okay."

He almost lost it and broke into choking sobs, but he held it together. "They took her."

"I know," I said, feeling my temper rise. "Over some drugs in the ceiling of our Tahoe? What the fuck, man?"

"I need to get those drugs back."

"I'll say you fucking do. Clyde, I'm so sorry, man."

"Thanks."

One man I did not want to be right then was Sean Griffin. Knowing Clyde's little girl was out there in the clutches of the dealers who owned the load in the Tahoe, I knew for a fact that Clyde would do anything to get the load back so he could get his daughter. Griffin did not want to mess with a live wire like Clyde.

"I got somewhat of a plan," he said. Clyde held out a rectangle of plastic. An I.D. I read it and holy shit—an FBI badge. The name said Stu Trumble. "Where the hell did you get that?"

"I borrowed it."

And the list of felonies grew longer. "What are you gonna do with it?"

"Get the drugs back. Then get my daughter."

I hoped like hell he was right and I loved the plan. Mostly because I saw a very familiar Tahoe pull into the parking lot right then.

41
SEAN

"Is that who we're supposed to meet?" I didn't answer. "Sean. Is that who we are supposed to meet?"

"I don't know, Linda. Probably. Just shut up a second."

Two guys sat in the front of an Infiniti. It looked like one was a doctor. I hoped they had cash, because all of a sudden I just wanted to get this over with. I was sweating everywhere. Even my balls were wet. "Stay here," I said.

I climbed out of the car and looked around. I'd chosen the parking lot at the Benjamin Franklin hotel. It was busy and I knew from a slight indiscretion a few years back when Linda and I had a bad fight, that it rented rooms by the hour. No one would think anything of a couple of cars parked for a short time. At least I hoped not.

I covered half the distance to the Infiniti and waited. The guy in green doctor's wear leaned over and said something to the driver. I hadn't brought a gun. What an idiot. I hadn't brought a gun. Everyone knows you take a gun to a drug deal. Sweat puddled in my flip flops. Second thoughts pinged around in my head. Mistake. Mistake. Mistake. I wiped the sweat from my eyes and waited.

The men in the Infiniti quit talking. Slowly, the passenger door opened. The doctor climbed out. He looked like a microwaved turd. Two black eyes and a bruised nose. What the fuck? The other guy, the little shit from the car place climbed out next. They both shambled toward me.

"You got it?" the doctor asked.

"Yeah. He's got it. Where the fuck is our money?" I jerked at the words. Linda had left the safety of the Tahoe and stood beside me.

"Linda, what the fuck?"

"I said where's our money?" Linda said again.

I moved to grab her arm, but she yanked it away.

The doctor cleared his throat. "Calm down, ma'am." Linda stopped and stared at him. He cleared his throat again. "I'm going to have to ask you to accompany my friend here to headquarters. I'll be taking over your vehicle."

My heart hammered in my chest. He held out his identification. FBI. It screamed at me from its little laminated cover. Holy fuck. Probably an undercover narc or some shit. I'd done it now. My stomach gurgled and for a horrifying minute I thought I was literally going to shit my pants. I didn't even know that was possible. Turns out, it is. People can actually be scared enough to shit their pants. I clenched and the feeling passed.

Linda stood beside me, her mouth hanging open. Her breath rasped in and out in a wheeze. At least if we were in prison I wouldn't have to listen to her breathing, or talking, or walking, or anything anymore.

"Fine," I said, holding out my wrists for cuffs. "I don't give a fuck anymore. Take me away. Get me away from her."

She rocked back like I'd slapped her. "Sean," she said. She said it real quiet too, like she was surprised I'd dare to hate her. Tough shit. I did. I hated her.

I stared at the cop in scrubs. "So what's with the disguise?"

The driver shuffled his feet and looked nervous. "We've been up all night, pal. No more talking. You've caused a lot of trouble for a lot of people. Get in the car. Now."

I jerked my head toward the Tahoe. "Keys are in it."

There was a sound like a car backfiring and bit of the parking lot puffed up in front of me. The sound came again and Linda fell to the ground.

Everything after that blurred. The FBI guy and his driver ran back to the Infiniti and jumped inside. Why hadn't they drawn their weapons and fired back?

Linda lay on the ground, moaning. "Get up," I said. "Get up!" Blood leaked from a spot on her side. Shit. I leaned down as more asphalt kicked up around us. "Linda. Get up. Move your ass. I don't want to die."

She grunted and pushed herself to her knees. "Fuck. You." she said, pushing my hands away as I tried to help her up. We limped to the Tahoe and climbed inside. A bullet pinged off the hood.

I slammed the car into reverse and whipped it around. I hit the gas as a bullet shattered the rear window.

I pulled out into traffic and sped way, wondering what the fuck we would do now.

42
SKEETER

Goddammit. I'm gonna get an earful for this. Don't shoot when you're high, Skeeter. You got no aim when you're high, Skeeter. Fuck.

It was a good goddamn plan, if I could have hit 'em. I got one, I know that. The woman. Same fatty who clocked me with the tray. Felt damn good to put a slug in her.

I watched them all get out of their cars and stand there in the open like a dumb-ass bridge game in the middle of a parking lot. Suburban fat-asses and those car rental jerk weeds. Sometimes I just fuckin' hate humanity.

I got to what I thought was a good vantage point. Kinda hard to find a good spot in this place. Not a lot of trees or other stuff to hide behind. Not where I could keep an eye on things at least. So maybe I was a little too far away. You know how you can get beer goggles and think a girl is fuckable even when in the cold light of day she's a greasy troll? Well, maybe I got meth goggles on and thought I could hit four targets from a distance that perhaps I was not quite the marksman for. And maybe my hand was a little shaky.

Either way, Corgan was gonna be pissed. And by the time I got back to my car, the bastards had scattered and I didn't see where they went. Shit. At least I got the woman.

43
BRENT

No way in hell I was going to lose that Tahoe from my sight. Clyde wasn't buckled in, and I don't think he even had is door closed yet when I punched it.

"Who the fuck was shooting?" I asked.

"I don't know." Clyde was watching the SUV burn rubber out of the parking lot, knowing that if we lost them and this whole deal went south, his daughter was in jeopardy. I know he wanted to tell me to speed up, to go after them, but he could see I was doing whatever I could to catch up.

We banged over a curb and landed in the street, trying to cut them off, but the Tahoe made almost a complete U-turn and tore out of the lot on the opposite side.

"Brent!" Clyde couldn't give detailed instructions, he was too panicked. His daughter might as well have been in the backseat screaming, "Daddy, Daddy. Don't let them take me."

I shot the Infiniti over the curb and back into the parking lot. I started to worry about the shocks, but I had no choice. We took out a bed of flowers and dented the front bumper pretty damn well as I crashed back down to pavement level off the strip of landscaping between the street and the lot. I was thankful for the nearly vacant early morning parking lot as I gunned it to follow the SUV.

"It must have been one of Corgan's men," Clyde said, still trying to figure the shooting. "Why the hell would he break it up right as we were about to get the thing back?"

"We didn't have any money," I said. "And that bitch didn't seem like she was going to leave without any."

"Oh, Jesus, I don't care. Just catch them. Don't let them get away."

I wasn't going to. The Tahoe's engine was big, sure, but ours was wasn't hauling around such a heavy load. We growled like a Lamborghini as we barreled after them.

"He was about to give up," Clyde cried out before punching the dash.

We hit the street on the far end of the lot and I could see the Tahoe veer around a corner a block away. Griffin drove like a drunk and the car fishtailed out before he wrestled control back. Let them roll the damn thing. We didn't need the vehicle—the actual SUV still belonged to us—all we needed was in that ceiling.

Down the straightaway I gave it all I had. I waited until I felt uncomfortable before I braked to make it around the corner I'd seen the SUV turn. The car gripped nicely on the pavement, a few early morning drivers swerving to get out of my way. Griffin was up ahead, moving fast. We were out of the beachside business area already, the trees around us filling in and the buildings becoming more spaced out. I chanced a look down and we were doing eighty-two.

Clyde worried his lip with his bottom teeth as he watched the wide-screen of the windshield like it was the most exciting and tense movie he'd ever seen.

I had to veer around one car between us and Griffin, but after that it was a straight shot right up his ass. Griffin didn't bother to turn or try to lose us in the maze of side streets. As criminals go, this guy was worse than we were.

I pulled up beside him, close enough to see him arguing with the woman who'd been shot. His wife. Quite different from the cuckolded nag I'd met in the rental office. I don't know when she'd grown a pair of balls, but I wish she hadn't.

"What do I do?" I asked.

"Ram him."

"Maybe you should flash him your badge. Tell him to stop."

"Run him off the road, goddammit."

Clyde reached for the wheel and tried to steer me into the SUV. We clipped the back panel, right behind his rear tire. The Tahoe was so much bigger than our car it barely flinched at the smack on the ass, but Griffin was such a panty-waste driver that he jerked the wheel and sent his car into a snake slither pattern across the yellow lines. I braked a little to back away from his wild side-to-side and got ready in case he righted the ship and I had to ram him again. I didn't have to.

OVER THEIR HEADS

The Tahoe squealed right and the front tire bit the soft shoulder. That did him in. Brake lights flared on and he slid off the road and into a ditch. I glided to a halt behind him and Clyde was out the door before my wheels stopped rolling.

44
CLYDE

I jumped from the car and strode to where the Tahoe had come to rest, nose down, in the ditch. Griffin was rubbing his neck as if he'd wrenched it when he went off the road. I opened his door and pulled him out by the ear. If there's one thing I learned from my fifth grade English teacher, it's that you can make a guy do anything if you get him by the ear.

Mr. Sean Griffin climbed out of the car without protest, whimpering the whole way. I twisted the ear for good measure and he grabbed my wrist as he started to sink to his knees. I shook him off and clocked him in the nose. Then I spun him around and slammed his face against the back seat window of the car so he could have a good look at his wife. She was writhing in the back seat, crying and bleeding all over the upholstery. She reached up and laid her palm on the window. It left a bloody streak when she pulled it away. Her mouth was working and her face was red. I noticed Griffin had turned the car off and it had to have been getting hot in there. It looked like Mrs. Griffin was yelling. At least we had that in common...we both had pissed off wives. I pushed his face into the glass. "Is this what you wanted, you fat fuck? Is this how you thought it would go down?"

"No. Oh God, I'm sorry. I'm so sorry."

I pulled the badge from my pocket and waved it in his face. "Speeding," I said, punching him in the back.

"We were getting shot at."

"Fleeing the scene of a shooting." I punched him again. "Not cooperating with an investigation."

"I'm cooperating. Oh God, I'm cooperating. My wife's been shot."

I punched him in the kidney and he crumpled to the ground. "Please don't hurt us. Oh God, please don't hurt us." I kicked him for good measure.

Brent was standing in the ditch looking at something in the distance. He looked like hell. He looked like he wanted to be somewhere else. Seeing him helped bring me back to where I needed to be, right here, thinking of my daughter. Griffin had his hand wrapped around my foot.

"Where are the keys?" I asked.

He just laid there, blubbering. I kicked him again with my free foot. "Where are the fucking keys?"

"In the ignition," he wheezed.

I moved around him and opened the back door, pulling the bleeding Mrs. Griffin out and letting her fall on top of her husband. I moved to get in the driver's seat.

"What do you want to do with these guys?" Brent asked, his voice quiet. He didn't get pissed very often, but when he did, his voice got quiet like that.

We needed to get off the road. We'd been parked here for a few minutes now. It would suck if a good Samaritan stopped by or, God forbid, a real cop. I blew out a breath. "Shit. Let them walk. She's not hurt so bad. Probably just a flesh wound."

"Probably," Brent said real quiet.

"Look," I said. "We're not killers. I don't care what you do with them. Don't hurt them any worse than they already are."

"What are you talking about?" Mrs. Griffin asked. "You're a cop."

God help me, I wanted to kick her too. "If you can get back to Richmond and check on the shop, I'd appreciate it. I don't even know if it is still standing. Let me take care of this last bit of business and then we'll talk, okay?"

He didn't say anything. He just stared at me.

I climbed in the Tahoe and tossed it into 4WD to get out of the ditch.

45
BRENT

I didn't want them in my car. He stank of flop sweat and she wouldn't stop making noises from the back seat. Clyde was right, we're not killers. I'm sure some people would have dumped them in a shallow grave out of revenge for what they tried to pull or to get rid of witnesses, but all we do is rent cars. I do, anyway. I don't dump bodies. So there I was, driving away to dump these two bodies back at a house in the suburbs, back with their two spoiled kids and their grandparents. I wondered if they'd gotten the larceny out of their systems.

The wife, Linda, sure talked a good game out there in the parking lot. Until she got shot, that is. Now she was grunting and whining like a dog who got run over by a car. I picked up a dog once after I saw it get clobbered by a minivan. I drove it to a vet and gave it over. They wanted me to pay for fixing it. I told them it wasn't my dog, I couldn't get involved. This wasn't my mess either and I was damn glad to be getting it over with. If that meant driving these two assholes who tried to hijack us back to their real lives so I could get back to mine, so be it.

"Hey listen," Sean started to say. "I wanted to apologize—"

"It's better if you don't say a goddamn word, Griffin." I started straight ahead, hands tense on the wheel and my voice quiet. "Only thing coming out of your mouth should be directions. And if you could get her to shut the fuck up too, that'd be nice."

He turned over the seat and spoke to her in a low tone. "Linda, please, keep it down. We'll be there in fifteen minutes and then we can get you taken care of."

She responded with a louder, more pained whine. She sounded like a cat in heat. She deserved it. I wasn't going to be the one to shoot her, or Sean, but I didn't feel the least bit bad she'd taken a bullet.

I might not have had a gun, but I couldn't resist poking the wound a little bit. "I bet a smelly car doesn't seem so bad right about now, does it?"

I checked for a reaction in the rear-view, but she kept right on writhing with her eyes closed. For the first time in twenty-four hours, I smiled.

46
SKEETER

The last snort stung like a bitch when it went up my nose. I was trying like hell to suck down even the most microscopic crystal. Damn near sucked my lungs inside out. The last bump is the worst. As much as that first bump is like the first smoke of the morning, only, like, times a million, the last bump with nothing else on the horizon is like getting punched in the face by a ball of barbed wire.

Important thing was I was speeding again. Maybe too fast. Back behind the wheel of my own car which I'd liberated from the hotel parking lot now that the cops had all gone home, I was thinking hard on how to rectify this situation. Lard-ass still had the dope. Car rental guys were still running around looking for him and I didn't get my chance to ride in as the hero and deliver the load and the heads of the jerks who tried to steal from us to Corgan. Guess I got a little ahead of myself on that count.

My brain buzzed with the throttle wide open. My connection to Brent was about all I had, only I didn't know where to find him when he wasn't at the shop. I could call Corgan and get info on where Clyde was at, but that would be explaining what went to shit at the meeting. And I could ask Corgan for some extra hands on this deal, but we'd have the same issue.

Guess I wasn't going as fast as I thought because some jackass in a red four door went blasting past me leaning on his horn and giving me the finger. I checked my Speedo and I was only doing about thirty in a forty-five zone, but still, you don't give me the finger unless you want it snapped off and shoved up your ass.

I gave my little four cylinder the beans and she whined like hell but started catching up. Pretty soon I was doing sixty in the forty-five zone. I'd see how he liked that.

I came up on his rear bumper and pawed through my glove

box until I found a Slayer CD. I pushed it in and cranked it up real loud. I wanted to sound real evil. With my windows rolled down I gunned it again and veered into the lane next to him. I could see him checking me out, a big old frat boy type from UVA or something. He gave me attitude again, but I noticed he didn't shoot me the finger or nothing this time. He realized he was dealing with a no bullshit kind of guy.

"Where's that finger now, punk?" I yelled across the lane between us. I doubt he could hear me over the Slayer. He slowed down to let me drift by him, all of sudden less concerned with pinning it right to the speed limit. I slowed down with him.

"Hey, you dropped something back there," I said. Then I flipped him the bird high and straight. He shot another one right back at me. Fucker. I swerved and knocked doors with him, two doors to four. Now he looked different. He grabbed the wheel with both hands, his finger back where it belonged. Well, shit, really it belonged up his ass, but I was driving so...

He started cursing me out. I couldn't hear a word of it but you can see it on someone's face when they're pissed and goin' off like that. I tapped him again and he jammed on his brakes to get away from me. I laughed my ass off and let him go. Out of habit I reached for another bump, like a cig after a good fuck. Forgot for a second I was out. It cooled my mood for a little bit, but at least I figured out where to go. If I had to find this Brent guy, the only place I knew to look for him was at the car rental place. I doubted he'd be there just hangin' around, but I did bet there would be some record of him. Employee file, paycheck stub, some shit. Something with his address on it.

Hell, anything was better than calling Corgan.

47
SEAN

The kid dumped us at the front sidewalk outside of Betty and Ernie's house. Linda leaned heavily on me as I limped toward the door. She was bleeding quite a bit, all over my shirt. For a wild minute I wanted to toss her to the ground and just take off, run anywhere. I didn't do it, of course. But I'd be lying if I said the thought hadn't crossed my mind.

I lugged her up the three steps to the porch and prayed that the front door was unlocked. Naturally it wasn't. I rang the bell and waited. When no one answered, I rang again and heard Ernie shouting from somewhere in the back of the house, "Betty, get the damn door."

After a minute, her sour face peeked out at us, turning from acrid to shocked in a fraction of a second. In another circumstance, I might have found her reaction comical. "Get out of the way, Betty, Linda's been shot."

"Oh Jesus, Jesus Christ in Heaven," she said, backing away. "Don't get anything on the carpet."

I dragged Linda into the bathroom and sat her on the toilet. I pulled washcloths from the cupboard and tossed them in the sink. "Get those wet with cold water," I barked at Betty.

"Those are my good washcloths, for company."

"Good. We're company."

Ernie called from the family room, "Who is it?"

Betty's hand fluttered about her throat. "It's...uh...Linda's been shot."

Linda moaned a little and blinked. I wanted to choke her. The sound of Ernie's heavy frame pounded down the hallway. "What the hell is this?" he asked.

He shoved me and Betty out of the way and knelt beside his daughter, pulling up her shirt to examine the wound. Betty wasn't good for anything at the moment, so I wet the washcloths and wrung them out in the sink. I waved them at

OVER THEIR HEADS

Betty. She hesitated and then stepped forward and tapped Ernie on the shoulder and handed them to him. He took them and placed them over the hole in Linda's side. The bullet had grazed her. Cutting a deep gash in her side, but as Ernie cleaned it up, it was obvious it wasn't deep.

"For Christ sakes, Linda," he grumbled. "It's a goddamn flesh wound. Sit up and stop the theatrics."

Her brow furrowed, but she stopped writhing and moaning.

He stood and shook his head, looking at me with the same disgust he always showed. "Mind telling me what this is all about?" he asked.

"I want to take a shower," Linda said. "I feel awful."

"What happened?" Betty demanded. "What are you involved in?"

Linda looked at me. "It was a hunter," she said. "We were in the woods and a hunter shot me."

No one said anything for a minute. The logical question would have been to ask why we hadn't called the cops, or 911. But Betty had never been one for dealing with hard questions and harder answers, so she just pursed her lips, nodded once, and then moved to help Linda undress.

I followed Ernie to the kitchen and poured myself a cup of coffee. Chad and Becky sat at the table, hunched over their bowls of cereal. "What happened to Mom?" Becky asked.

Ernie glared at me as he answered her. "She cut her side."

He jerked his head at me and I followed him through the kitchen and onto the deck where we wouldn't be overheard.

"It's not hunting season," he said.

"No."

"What the hell is going on, Sean? What the hell is going on?"

Becky opened the door. "Gramps, is it okay if I bake cookies? Any time Mom gets stressed, she likes to eat a lot of cookies. I mean a LOT."

"Sure, kid. Go ahead." He turned back to me. "Well?"

48
CLYDE

I pulled into the nearest gas station so I could call Corgan. I smelled like I hadn't showered in days. I parked next to a gas pump and climbed out. The bloody hand print from Mrs. Griffin was somewhat hard to see in the shade. I opened the back door and went to work on it with a squeegee. A guy in a Mercedes took the pump in front of mine. When he climbed out he gave me a thumb's up. "Just getting off your shift, Doc?"

I tried to give him a smile and something resembling a nod.

"Cool. What line are you in?" His eyes rolled over the bruising on my face and for a second he looked like he wanted to change his mind about asking.

What line was I in? What the hell did that mean? Green scrubs. I looked like a doctor. "ER," I said, thinking fast. "Just helped deliver a baby."

"Nice. I'm an anesthesiologist." He smiled like I should be impressed.

"Cool," I said. I climbed back in the Tahoe and parked in the spot closest to the front door. I knew I should probably eat something, but I couldn't think of anything but getting my baby girl back and somehow trying to make things right with Madeline again. I didn't know if my marriage was over or not. Christ I hoped not. I didn't know what the fallout would be from the deal with Corgan, but after this I was done. I was done forever. God just let me get through this.

I wasn't going to eat anything. I didn't know if I'd ever eat again.

I punched in Corgan's number and waited.

"Mr. McDowd. How nice to hear from you."

"I've got the Tahoe."

"Great. I knew you could do it if I motivated you. I'm all about motivation."

No shit. "How's my daughter?"

"She's fine, kid, just fine. Lot of hair on this girl. And a nice set of lungs, too."

I pressed my lips together and waited for the wave of nausea I was feeling to pass.

"Meet me at the Waffle House by the beach."

"Waffle House."

"It's brunch time, my friend. Come on in and let me buy you some pancakes while you hold your baby girl."

I pointed the Tahoe through the still quiet streets of downtown Virginia Beach. In a couple of hours the beach would be crowded and everyone would be half drunk by noon. I passed the diners and clubs that had probably changed hands a half dozen times in the last fifteen years. The one establishment that hadn't changed since my college days was the Waffle House. It probably had the same matted carpet, the same menu, and probably the same waitresses—older, a little softer and a little harder at the same time.

Despite the blast of the AC, I was sweating. I pulled into a parking space and tried to catch my breath. I was about to meet my daughter. It wasn't lost on me that our first meeting would be me delivering drugs to Corgan to get her back to her mother. I was done with this. After this drop, finished. No more. It ended now. I was done being a goddamn mule. I wanted out.

I didn't know if I had a business to go back to. I didn't know if I had a marriage anymore. The sun had been up for a few hours now, and the chances of the FBI noticing that a badge was missing were pretty good. One way or another there would likely be jail time, maybe prison.

None of that changed the fact that right now I was a father. First things first...get my baby girl back.

I took a deep breath and swallowed. I didn't remember my last meal, my last drink of water. I rested my head against the seat and willed myself to move. My eyes slid to the ceiling panel and I felt a little reassured, knowing this was the end of the road. I felt my mouth curve up in a smile, the first I'd had in a couple of days. I reached over to give the ceiling fabric a pat to reassure myself the familiar solidity of the bricks was still there.

It billowed under my hand like an empty sack. My heart seized. I reached across and pulled at the corner. It came away free in my hand, the fabric hanging like torn tarp. That fucker Griffin had taken it all.

What would Corgan do now? What would he do to my daughter?

I needed more time. Had any of Corgan's men seen me? Probably so. I was sure he had men watching the parking lot, waiting to grab me. I tucked the fabric back in place and sat for a minute. Corgan and another man appears outside of the Waffle House and ambled over to the Tahoe. I sat still and tried not to look as panicked as I felt. They climbed into the backseat. A third climbed into the Pontiac in the next space.

"Drive," Corgan said.

I had no idea if they knew the roof panel was empty. I just drove. My baby made small smacking and cooing sounds. In the rear-view, I could see a tuft of dark hair peeking out from a blanket.

"Your baby needs her diaper changed," Corgan said. "She is a big eater, I'll tell you that much." He used a fat finger to stroke her hair.

"Where are we going?" I managed.

He directed me to a warehouse district.

Naturally.

It's always a warehouse district. This was where they'd put a bullet between my eyes, smash my baby's head with a brick and leave us to be discovered by the homeless. Or maybe they'd just leave me and sell her on the black market.

"This monkey could have taken a shower," Corgan's spare covered his nose as he spoke.

"Indeed," Corgan said. "Pull over here."

I parked the car and turned to face Corgan. "Look."

"Get out," he said.

I climbed out and stood on shaking legs. Corgan climbed out too. "Here she is, as promised."

"You don't understand," I said. But he was placing her into my arms.

"I'm a reasonable man. I mean your child no harm unless you cross me. See how reasonable I am?"

The man in the Pontiac climbed out and stood beside his car, arms folded in front of him.

OVER THEIR HEADS

I looked down at my daughter. She had dark eyes, like her mother and a head full of dark hair. Her tiny pink hands were balled into fists at her cheeks. She was the tiniest thing I'd ever seen and the most beautiful.

"It's empty," Corgan's thug reported.

I tore my gaze from my daughter and met Corgan's eyes—eyes that had gone cold and hard.

49
SEAN

The house smelled like chocolate chip cookies. I shouldn't have been hungry after everything that had been going on, but my stomach rumbled audibly. Ernie glared at me.

After Linda got out of the shower, her side bandaged and her mood a little better, we showed her parents where the coke was hidden, in a plastic bin under the bed in our room. Now we were on the back deck again, where we could speak freely.

"We were trying to sell it back," I said.

"Well of all the..." Betty said. "Linda, we raised you better than that. I cannot believe what this man has talked you into."

"Looks like a lot of coke," Ernie said. He was leaning back in his chair and rubbing his chin, thinking.

"It was in the ceiling of the car."

"We found it by accident," Linda supplied. "We weren't involved in anything illegal."

She looked at me as if daring me to tell them about how I'd financed our vacation. Yeah, I was going to have to re-think this whole marriage thing when we were done. Mostly when I looked at her now I wanted to punch something.

Ernie stood and opened the liquor cabinet and poured two drinks. He returned to his chair, handing me a glass as he did so. "I want to hear every single detail of this."

I had just told him everything, out on the deck, but the son of a bitch wanted to hear it all again. So what if I'd held a few things back before. He studied me with those razor sharp eyes and I knew he knew that there was more to what I'd told him before. About Detroit. About my brother's business and getting screwed out of what was mine.

"Start at the beginning and leave nothing out." He leaned forward and rested his hands on his knees. Then he gestured to his wife. "And you," he said, "keep your mouth shut while he's talking. I need to hear what he has to say. And this time I want the whole story."

So I cleared my throat and started at the beginning...the very beginning, back in Michigan when I took what was mine from my brother and his partner.

50
SKEETER

I ran my car over something. No idea what it was. Could have been a person, I guess. Probably a cat or a raccoon or a possum. Some fuckin' thing that didn't know no better. That's some Darwin shit right there.

I didn't see it. Felt the bump. My eyes had gone blurry, my brain a little hazy—not at the edges like when you're tired—but right down the middle like I had my own personal Charlie Brown dark cloud in the center of my brain shooting lightning and raining until my thoughts were water-logged and slow. It happens on the comedown. The God. Damned. Come. Down.

The crystal I'd scored had been cheap rocks. If the good shit is diamonds, these were rhinestones. The high was wearing off before my nose even stopped dripping into the back of my throat. Could have been all the damn thinking I was doing. Working out a new plan, wondering what would happen to the shitheel once I found him. All the shitheels.

I saw a sign for a rest area. At least I think that's what it was. Damn thing blurred right past me and didn't have the decency to look in focus. I merged over and took the exit anyway. I'd been right. Rest area to stretch your legs, take a piss, have a picnic or some other shit.

Two Coke machines sat inside the little overhang right outside the shitter. I had to feed a crumpled dollar into the fuckin' thing six times before it would take, and even then I still owed another seventy-five cents. For a goddamn Coke. Shit.

I flipped open my phone and dialed Evvie, my girlfriend. She was always really cool when I took off for work. Never gave me shit about it, never asked too many questions. But since this trip was dragging into extra days, I figured I'd give her the update.

I don't keep a calendar or nothing, but I think I caught her on the rag.

"Where the fuck have you been?"

"Workin', baby. I told you that."

"You was supposed to be back yesterday. You missed spaghetti night."

"Shit, darlin', I'm sorry. Things are gettin' crazy over here. It's gonna be another day or so."

"Another day?"

I worked hard to keep my cool. She had no right to give me shit like that. I tried like hell to take the high road.

"Two tops," I said.

"Skeeter, I swear you better get one of them iPhones so's I can text you. Everybody uses texting these days. I wouldn't have to wait until you think to call me."

"Them things are, like, four hundred bucks. Fuck that. I'm calling you now, ain't I? Why do I need to text you?"

"Because that's what couples do." She said like she was talking to a real dumb-ass. High road. High. Road.

"Oh, you mean, like, sexy pictures and shit?"

"No goddammit. I want you to tell me where you are, when you're coming home. Stuff like that. It's not for taking titty pictures with. It's called a smart phone, not a dumb-ass phone."

High road was a dead end.

I sucked in one deep breath and tried not to raise my voice. "Now you listen to me, you stupid cunt, you call me a dumb-ass again and I'll cut those titties right off your chest and you won't be taking pictures for no one. I'm fuckin' callin' you now. You better like it 'cause that's all you're getting. And when I do get home you better shape up your fucking attitude."

I snapped the phone shut before she could say something stupid to piss me off even more. I wanted like hell to smash the damn phone into pieces and crush it with my boot, but I might still need to call Corgan on it so I held it together. I needed something though, so I took out my gun and shot the Coke machine. Three times. It leaked dark Coke like blood from the three holes. Well, I think one was Mountain Dew.

A mother and her daughter came rushing out of the ladies room and ran to their car. Little girl didn't even have time to pull up her panties. The mom blocked her like a human shield. Now, that's a good momma for you. Put yourself in harm's way for your kids. I respected that. More than my mom ever did for me.

I slurped down the rest of the Coke can in one chug and crushed can underfoot, then I got in the car and kept on for the airport.

51
BRENT

When I got to the shop the car had been pulled out of the hole in the wall. The inside looked like someone's guts in the middle of a transplant. Like, the new liver hadn't been put in yet. Just a big empty space and a lot of mess around it. The front (formerly) glass wall was crisscrossed with yellow police tape. Pulling in I saw one cop car left over and, as I got out of my car, I could see a lone cop standing in the rental shop, picking through the rubble.

I stuck a piece of gum in my mouth, chewed it fast for a dozen chews, then spit it out. Best I could do without a toothbrush. My B.O. was unfortunately inoperable. I did my best to smooth down my hair in the side view mirror, but if this cop was worth a damn he'd know I'd been through a rough night and day.

My best bet was to play dumb. Easy enough. I'd been feeling like a right idiot for the past forty-eight hours. I stepped forward and let my jaw drop at the sight of it all.

"Holy hell. What happened to the shop?"

The cop looked up, moved a hand to the pistol on his hip, then relaxed when he saw me. "Can I help you?"

"Yeah, I work here." I looked around at the damage. It wasn't hard to act stunned. "I guess I used to work here."

"Are you the owner?"

"No. Just a worker." I kicked a small pile of glass with the toe of my shoe. "Jesus..."

"We've been trying to reach the owner all day."

"Oh, Clyde just had a baby. His wife did, I mean. He hasn't been around." I shook my head like it was all too much, which it was. "He isn't going to like this." I looked up at the cop. "What happened?"

It was a good chance to see what they knew and didn't know. If he mentioned Corgan's name, or Griffin's, it would only be a matter of time before he got to mine. I started liking the fact that we were standing next to an airport because my next move was to buy a ticket to anywhere and leave this place for good. Let the lovers have Virginia.

"Someone drove an SUV through the front window of the establishment. We're working on a motive."

"We don't keep any cash on hand. Everything is done by credit card these days. Any idea who?"

"It was empty when we got here. Someone from another rental counter called it in."

I looked around, nodded my head. "Well, I'll be."

"Do you have some I.D. on you, sir?"

"Oh, uh, yeah." I handed over my license. If he didn't know anything, I had nothing to hide. The thing I did want to keep from him were my car keys, which I'd come back to get. If they started to do any inventory or CSI-type stuff on the rental business they'd see that the Infiniti wasn't rented to anyone. I didn't want to get pulled over in a car now associated with a crime scene. So I needed to find a way to dig through the mess and find the ruins of the drawer where I always put my junk when I worked. I hated that Clyde made me wear the pleated Dockers and I hated more the way my keys jangled and rubbed in those knee-deep pockets. I kept too much shit on my key ring, I knew that. Everyone gives out those little plastic cards with the bar codes on them—for the gym, the club at the grocery store, the library. I had too many of those and the little bottle opener I got at the Redskins game that time and then the keys themselves. Car, house, back door to the house, rental shop, some key that used to work in the van I had a few years ago. I never got around to clearing that off. So, yeah, it was a big chunk of noisy metal in my pocket, so I always took them out and put them in the drawer just like how I took them out and tossed them in the same spot on the kitchen counter every time I got home.

Home. A place I couldn't get to without those keys.

I started shuffling around, moving debris with my shoes as I edged close to where the drawer at least used to be. It also put me closer to the cop. He handed me back my license.

"Sorry I can't really let you snoop around too much. It's still a crime scene after all."

"Yeah, yeah," I said, still trying to snoop as much as he'd allow. "What happened to the car? You said a car went through the front?"

"SUV. It's at impound being swept for prints."

I toed over a fiberboard hunk of the former counter. The drawer had to be in the pile I was standing on. The one Skeeter had plowed directly into. "Well, you'll find my prints on pretty much every car in the lot. Hope that doesn't mean you think I did it." I smiled at him. He didn't smile back.

"Should I think you did it?"

My face fell. "No, no. I was just...I was kidding. I mean, my prints are probably on all the cars. It's my job after all. I mean I move them, I clean them out, I do a lot of—"

"Relax." He looked more closely at my face. "You cut yourself shaving?"

"Huh?" My hand went to my face by instinct. "Oh, yeah. Probably. I use an electric but the battery was dead so I broke out the old twin blade. Guess I'm out of practice." I smiled and laughed like an insurance salesman. Talking myself into a jail cell.

"Yeah. So out of practice you knicked yourself on the forehead a few times."

He was matching the tiny cuts and scrapes on my face with the pattern of flying glass and flying SUVs. I didn't like the math he was calculating.

"Is it true that a criminal returns to the scene of the crime?" My lame idea of changing the subject. I couldn't do worse if I gave him the license plate of the Tahoe.

"Very rarely," he said. He squinted at me. "But it does happen."

52
CLYDE

I tried to speak with a tongue that was stuck to the roof of my mouth. Sweat ran into my eyes, stinging them. Corgan took my baby and held her for a minute. "Here, Paulie," he said to one of the guys. "You'd better take her because if you don't...if someone doesn't take this kid from me...I AM GOING. TO. CRUSH. HER FUCKING HEAD. WITH MY BOOT."

The baby screamed and I thought in that second that she had her mother's lungs, that she was a hell of a yeller. Chip off the old lady. I still couldn't speak. Corgan didn't look grandfatherly any more. He looked maniacal. A ball of spit had formed on his lower lip as he screamed and now, as he turned to talk to me, I watched it go from bottom lip to upper lip, a tiny, white spit ball. I fought the urge to giggle.

"I imagine you have something you want to say." He raised his eyebrows.

"They were gone when I got to the Waffle House. I didn't know the stash was gone. I didn't have any idea. I just got the car back and the family...the couple..." The baby kept screaming. I couldn't focus on what he was saying, I just kept watching that spit ball.

"Ah yes. This couple I've been hearing about." He clenched and unclenched his fists. "I'd really like to meet them."

Paulie was shushing my daughter, patting her bottom. I wanted to put a bullet in his brain.

"Great. I'll take you there. We'll go and get them."

"Excellent idea. What's their address?"

"I, well, I don't have it on me."

He wrinkled his nose and smiled a little. "I'm sure we can find it. Now," he clapped his hands once and rubbed them together, "I find a cigar helps to calm me down. If you'll excuse me, please."

He accepted a long cigar from one of his men and pulled a

cigar clip from his pocket. He cut off the end as he walked a ways in the distance. He motioned for Paulie and the baby to stay back, gesturing to the cigar, like he didn't want her exposed to the smoke. That was something, right? A guy worried about a baby inhaling smoke couldn't turn around and murder her, right?

He nodded to the other two and then moved toward me. I was caught between wanting to run, wanting to fight, and just wanting everything to be over. They went for my gut first. It's always the gut. A guy can't fight back after getting the wind knocked out of him. It's all he can do to stand upright. They stayed away from my face, but everything else seemed to be fair game. My bruised ribs broke this time. I tried to breathe in and felt the ends of bone rubbing together. Still they punched me. Back, sides, nuts, sides again. I fell to the ground and curled up as tight as I could. I fell asleep to the sound of my baby crying.

53
SKEETER

Sometimes I'm a goddamn genius.

I pulled into the parking lot past the airport, the one with all the car rental places. Right away I saw the ruined shell of Clyde's place after I'd destroyed it. Made me grin real wide, I tell you what. Almost as much as when I saw the king shitheel, Brent, standing in the rubble.

As sluggish as I was the last few miles into Richmond, seeing him standing there got my blood moving again. Almost as much as if I'd had a fresh bump up the ol' snooter.

Like I said, super genius.

Only one problem—a cop standing with him. But like the old philosopher Ice Cube once said—Fuck tha police.

Brent was my ticket. Things had gotten so screwed up in this deal that nothing short of me walking in with all these jerks' heads on a platter would keep me from losing my job with Corgan. And when you get dismissed from Corgan's organization there's no farewell party, no severance package and no gold watch. Just a bullet in the back and don't let the shovel hit you in the ass on the way into your shallow grave.

No way was I gonna let anyone or anything stop me from getting Brent and keeping him this time. No way.

I parked a safe distance away because I didn't want them to see me walking up. Not until I wanted them to. I weaved my way through the rows of parked cars and out to the front of the building. I wanted to come in the same way I did when I was driving that big ass SUV through the glass. I had to duck under the yellow tape and my feet crunching over glass let them know I was there. Brent saw me first.

"That's the guy. He drove through the front." He pointed at me like he saw a ghost.

The cop had been giving him the business, I think. He had a notebook open and the page was almost full. The pinched furrow of his eyebrows told me the cop wasn't buying whatever bullshit Brent was shoveling.

"That's the guy?" the cop asked.

"Yeah. His name is—"

I drew my gun from behind my back and shot the cop between the eyes. Well, okay, it wasn't dead center or anything. It hit off to the right and took out a big chunk of skull. From right above his arched eyebrow back to where his hairline had receded to.

A good deal of blood got on Brent because he had been moving behind the cop for protection like a little girl who thinks she's seen the boogeyman.

So I said, "Booo."

I bent over and took the cop's handcuffs from him and turned to Brent.

"Let's go," I said.

The pussy was still standing there all in shock and totally still. Cop blood dripped down his face and he didn't even have the sense to wipe it off.

"I said let's go."

"Where are we going?" he asked.

"You're gonna help me out. In case you didn't notice this whole thing has gone to shit. Finding you here was the best luck I've had in a week."

I pushed on his shoulder to get him moving, motivating him along with the gun. We left the cop in a pile of broken glass and fallen road maps of the greater Richmond area.

I brought Brent to my car, the pussy still too stunned to say anything. I put him in the passenger seat and cuffed his hand to the door handle so he wouldn't get any ideas of trying to bail out once we got rolling. I was pretty sure he wasn't gonna try anything after he saw me shoot a cop in the face. What can I say? I was amped up.

"Where are we going?" he asked.

"First things first, I need to go see a guy."

I knew an old dealer in downtown Richmond. Pretty sure he was still in business. We were headed to see him either way. After this little bit of good news, I deserved a reward.

"Okay, wait, wait, wait," he said.

"No, don't wait, wait, wait. We finish this now. Shit's gone on too long."

"But you don't understand."

I backhanded him with the butt of the gun. Missed his nose but cracked his teeth pretty good. That shut him up. I cranked the car to life and realized I'd left the Slayer playing in the CD. Had it turned up pretty fucking loud, too. We both jumped. I smiled, but turned it down a little. I'd see my guy downtown, get a little energy to make it through to the end of this thing. And if shitheel started talking again, I'd just crank up the metal.

54
SEAN

I stared at Ernie, waiting for him to say something to me. He got up and poured another drink. He tossed it back and his throat worked like he was trying not to gag. Linda sat on the sofa with her hand pressed to her bandaged side. Betty was shaking her head like one of those bobble-head dolls. Back and forth, back and forth, with her lips pursed like she was smelling a fart.

I wanted to go home. To Detroit. I'd rather deal with my brother and his partners than deal with Linda's father. Married sixteen years and he still made me feel like a pimply teenager caught with my hand up his daughter's top.

"Come with me," Ernie said, setting his glass down. When Betty and Linda rose to follow, he held out a hand. "Just Sean. You two stay here."

We passed through the kitchen where Becky was just unloading a pan of cookies onto a plate. I picked one up as we passed and gave her a wink. She frowned in response.

Ernie led me down the basement stairs. He had to duck his head as he moved, weirdly reiterating how much bigger than me he was. The basement was old and musty, but he kept a desk against the wall in the back. An old green leather recliner sat in the middle of the room with a pedestal-style ashtray beside it. A bin of old magazines sat in one corner. I pegged them for Playboys. A gun rack hung above the desk and he pulled down two of the four rifles that rested there, setting them on the desk.

He opened one of the desk drawers and pulled out a metal box. He unlocked it with a key from his pocket and pulled out the .45 resting inside. He also pulled out spare clips and boxes of cartridges for the rifles.

"What are we doing, Ernie?" I hated the sound of my voice. The bare cement walls made me sound like I was talking in a locker room.

He shoved a clip into the .45 and tucked it in the back of his jeans. Then he picked up a rifle and handed it to me, motioning that I should load it.

"I figure we got two choices," he said. "We can go to the cops. Or we can give the drugs you stole back to whoever they belong to." He rested the rifle in his arms and stared at me. "Now, cops will arrest you. No doubt about that. You took the drugs without the intention of giving them back. Because you're a loser who is married to my daughter."

I couldn't take my eyes off the gun in his arms. What was his plan? Get me to hold one gun while he held the other and then shoot me, claiming self-defense? Surely not. I was, as he so astutely pointed out, married to his daughter.

"What's the second option?" I asked.

He gave me a tight smile. "We find the guys this stuff belongs to and give it back. You get out. Leave my daughter and her kids with me. We don't see you again. Ever."

55
BRENT

I could feel some of the cop's blood on my face. The wet droplets I felt splash my cheek when this crazy bastard shot him at the rental place had dried now and itched like tiny scabs on my skin. I didn't want to scratch though because the blood would have gone under my fingernails. I could only reach my face with one hand anyway, the other one was cuffed to the door.

Skeeter seemed manic. His eyes wouldn't focus and I would not have picked him as my designated driver, yet there I was with this crank-head lunatic running the show.

I tried to reason with him: "Look, man, it's over. Clyde has the Tahoe. He's already met up with Corgan by now."

"Shut up. Goddamn, how many times I gotta tell you to shut up."

"I'm just trying to let you know the deal is over. Everything's put back right."

He punched me. Luckily it was a blind side shot and his loosely balled up fist only glanced off my cheek. We were in some dark corner of downtown Richmond I didn't recognize and from the look on Skeeter's face, he didn't either.

"I know it's here somewhere..." He stared at street signs as he drove slowly through intersections and drifted through stop signs.

"If you just call Corgan—"

He swung at me again, missing me mostly. He clipped the tip of my jawbone and it slammed my teeth together and made me bite my tongue. I cursed loudly and jerked my cuffed hand to put it to my mouth, forgetting for a second it was otherwise occupied. Skeeter swung the car to a stop at the curb outside a two story colonial that had seen better days—probably in actual colonial times.

Skeeter leaned over me and unlocked the handcuff that was clamped to the door. I knew I didn't want to go into that house, even if I didn't know what was inside. I thought for a second maybe he listened to me and was letting me go, but then he looped the chain of the cuffs through the door handle and clipped my other hand into the cuff, locking both my hands in place. His breath stank. His body stank. His ears were dirty. I was at least a little bit grateful when he leaned away from me, hands cuffed or not.

"Wait here," he said with a laugh as he practically bolted out the door. So I sat there, tongue stinging, wrists aching, head pounding and without a thing to do about any of it. Just when I thought this mess was over...

I heard the hum of my cell phone on vibrate. I twisted in my seat, feeling the buzz against my thigh. My hands wouldn't move anywhere close to allowing me access to my front pocket. I didn't know who it was, but if I could get to that phone I could ask for help. Not that I'd know where to tell them to come find me. But if I could only reach...the buzzing stopped.

I leaned my head against the window and let loose a long sigh.

Five minutes later Skeeter was back. He hadn't showered in there, that's for sure.

"My phone rang," I said. "I bet it was Clyde. He'll tell you it's all set now. Maybe it was Corgan, even."

"The fuck you talkin' about?" Skeeter was digging through the glove box for something.

"When you were inside my phone rang."

"Why didn't you answer it, dumb-ass?" He leaned back in his seat, his hand clamped around something small.

"Because you handcuffed me to the fucking door." I braced for another punch, weak as it may come, but Skeeter was too busy with his little prize—a glass pipe. "Aw, shit, you're not going to smoke crack in here are you?"

He gave me one crooked eye. "If I was, it ain't none of your fuckin' business."

"Look, just let me out. You don't even have to drop me back at the airport, I'll get a cab from here. We're all done on this deal. We never need to see each other again."

He was ignoring me. He packed three small crystals like rock candy into the bulb of the pipe. "Y'see sometimes I snort it. It's faster that way. You can grab a bump on the go real good with a snort. But it stings and it makes your eyes water. Smoking is a much more dignified way, don't you think? Great men smoked pipes. Sherlock Holmes, Abraham Lincoln, probably some other presidents."

"I don't think Lincoln smoked a pipe and even if he did it wasn't a crack pipe."

He gave me both crooked eyes this time, staring over the globe of the pipe. "I didn't realize I was in the car with a fuckin' history teacher."

He flicked his thumb on a lighter and I braced for a car full of smoke sure to get me a contact high—which I did not want—when my phone buzzed again.

"Oh, there. There. You hear it? Get my phone. I bet it's Clyde. Answer it. Come on."

I shoved my hip out so he could see the pocket where the vibrations were coming from. Annoyed, he lifted his thumb off the lighter, pulled the pipe down into one hand and dug through my pocket for my phone. He looked at the caller I.D. and pressed a button.

"The fuck you want?"

Clyde's voice. "Brent? Who is this?"

"It's someone who doesn't have time to answer a lot of fool questions."

"Skeeter?" He mumbled 'Shit,' under his breath. "Give the phone to Brent. I need to get a phone number for Griffin."

Skeeter looked at me. For a second I had no idea why Clyde would be calling me for that number, then I remembered. "In my back pocket," I blurted.

"This is all some sick game to get me to feel you, up you fuckin' homo."

"No, it's on the rental agreement. It's in my back pocket, left side."

Clyde could hear me and he pleaded with Skeeter. "Please, Skeeter. I'm here with Corgan. We need that number."

The mention of Corgan's name kicked Skeeter into gear. Only when Skeeter was wrist deep in my back pocket did it register that if Clyde was with Corgan and they needed Griffin's number, that was bad news.

56
SEAN

I didn't know where we were going. I didn't know what the plan was. Ernie just climbed in his truck and started driving. It was twenty minutes of silence before he pulled into the Virginia Beach Gun Club.

"Sit here and shut the fuck up," he said. "I gotta get more ammo."

We could have gone to Bass Pro Shops, I wanted to tell him, but I just nodded. Fucker wanted me to leave my family. My wife and kids.

My wife and kids. Did I really care? I sat for a minute and chewed on that. Becky, Chad, Linda. They could all stay here. I could go back to Detroit alone. Free. No more tuna casseroles. No more tater tots with green beans. No more Linda.

Ernie emerged from the building with several boxes of cartridges and clips. He climbed in the truck just as my phone rang. "Put it on speaker," he said.

I did as I was told. "Hello."

"Hello. Is this Sean Griffin?" Whoever it was sounded out of breath.

Ernie gave me a nod, like it was okay with him if I answered. "Yeah," I said. "This is Sean Griffin. Who is this?"

"You've got what I want."

Somewhere behind the voice, someone moaned. I also thought I heard the sound of a baby crying.

The connection went fuzzy. "Hello?" I said again.

"I'm here," the voice said. "Not going anywhere."

"Yes. We have your stuff," I said again.

"Good. We'll let you live if you return it. Don't return it and we'll make sure that the limited number of days you have left will be spent in agony."

I swallowed hard. Ernie took the phone from me.

"Listen here, you fuckwits. We have what you want and we'll

gladly sell it back to you for a price. One hundred thousand. Cash."

My mouth fell open. Ernie hadn't been there when they opened fire on us, but his daughter was back at his house with the bullet hole in her side as a testament to what these guys thought of folks who interfered in their business.

The sound of the baby crying grew louder, until it was a shriek. A man's voice rose with it, shouting. Sounded almost like begging. The crack of a gunshot came next followed by silence.

"Hello?" Ernie said.

"Yes. I'm so sorry. We'll have to call you back." The line went dead.

57
SKEETER

Once I'd had a few good pulls on the pipe and got my head right, I could think. Brent, the square asshole, was off in the corner holding his breath as long as he could and then letting it out in a big gasp like he'd just come up from the deep or something. Fuckin' annoying. It disturbed my thinking and ruminating.

Thinking stuff like: if they're going for another meet up with this Griffin jerk-off, why ain't I invited? This is my deal, right? Griffin is driving my Tahoe, right? I should be the one to get it back.

And if they're meeting with Griffin, then Brent was full of shit when he told me the deal was done and the drugs were back with Corgan, nestled right up to his ball sack safe and sound.

He gasped again. "Can you roll down my window, please?"

"No, I can't. It's hot out there." I sparked the lighter again.

"I can't breathe."

I held in my lungful, let it work its magic, then let it out. "I can breathe just fine." I let the high settle on my brain. Felt good—like pop rocks in a can of Coke. "So, you gonna admit you were lying to me?"

He exhaled. "What?"

"Clyde don't have the dope. Why would he be calling to get that guy's number if he had it?"

"I don't...I don't know." He sucked in more air and went under for a deep dive again.

"It's 'cause they're still trying to find him, that's why."

He blasted out his lungful of air. Really fuckin' annoying. "But Clyde drove away in the Tahoe."

"So?"

"So that's where the drugs were."

"Right, dumb-ass—were. The drugs were there. Now they're

somewhere else. On the street, up Griffin's ass, who the fuck knows."

Brent held his breath. I tried to think. No matter where the drugs were, I needed to be in on that meeting. Corgan would never see me as anything more than a delivery boy if I didn't finish this one out. I'd have to give Corgan a call. Yeah, call him directly and tell him why I should—

He broke the surface again and panted for breath. Motherfucker broke my concentration.

"Hey, asshole." I shot him in the foot. "I'm trying to think over here."

58
CLYDE

Corgan used my phone to call Griffin, his voice going from amiable to menacing in a flash. I couldn't really focus on what he was saying. One of the thugs was holding my baby, and he was doing it wrong. She was crying. I needed to hold her and let her know that I would get her home safe. "Give her here," I said.

"Fuck off." He moved away from me. Corgan gave us a look that spoke volumes.

"Give me my daughter," I said.

He shifted and she started to wail. I reached for her but the second thug grabbed me and tossed me to the ground. He put his boot on my chest. Corgan fired a warning shot that kicked up dust next to my knee. The baby screamed.

"I'm so sorry. We'll have to call you back," Corgan said.

59
BRENT

I stepped on a bee once. In my bare feet. Stung the bottom of my foot. I thought that hurt at the time. It didn't hurt at all, it turns out.

"You motherfucking shot me." My head banged against the window as I bucked in my seat trying to escape the pain. I yelled through gritted teeth for what felt like a really long time. My foot sparked and jumped at the end of my leg, the pain coming in sharp jolts like a line of a thousand army ants had crawled into my shoe and were feasting on my flesh.

"Aw, quit whining," Skeeter said.

I know I set out into this thing with all intentions of not hurting anyone, but if I'd have been able to reach his gun right then, I'd have gladly shot him in his stupid, pockmarked, peach fuzzed face.

"I need a hospital."

"No, you don't."

I lifted my foot. It nearly made me pass out, not only from the pain but from seeing the ragged hole in my shoe rimmed with red on top and dangling bits of stuff out the bottom. Bits of my flesh and probably the bones of my foot. There was a goddamn hole all the way through my foot.

Even Skeeter could see things did not look good.

"Okay, shit." He punched the dashboard like he was the one who was being put out. "If only you'd shut up like I told you to."

I let my foot down gently. Nothing I did helped the pain. I started hyperventilating. Short breaths that did nothing to fill my lungs.

"Alright, alright, calm the fuck down. I know a guy."

"A (breathe) (breathe) (breathe) guy?"

"Yeah, like a doctor." Skeeter dropped the car in gear. He actually looked more lucid to drive after a half dozen hits on the pipe than he did before.

"(breathe) Like (breathe) (breathe) a doctor?"

"It's this or I kick you the fuck out here."

I kept silent and slumped against the door, trying to control my breathing.

"Yeah," he said. "Thought so."

This was not a sanitary facility. It looked like a house in foreclosure. Scraggly lawn, torn screens in the windows, a few missing bricks in the facade. And Skeeter didn't even help me to the door. I had to hop behind him like an idiot. I almost tumbled into the dead shrubs more than once. By the time I got to the door I was breathing hard and the steady trickle of blood from the bottom of my foot had started again.

An old guy answered the door.

"Mister Gene," Skeeter said like they were old pals. The look on Mr. Gene's face said otherwise. "Got a patient for you. Put it on Corgan's tab."

Hearing Corgan's name was enough to make the old man open the door wide enough for me to hop through. He watched me pass by with a curious expression, but he didn't offer to help either.

In what used to be a dining room Mr. Gene waved me over to a table. I sat on the edge while he flicked on lights.

"So what happened?" he said, pulling on half glasses to examine my foot more closely.

"I got shot." I figured I didn't need to explain by whom.

He leaned his head back to get a glimpse through the full power of his lenses. "That so?" He turned my ankle which hurt like he was twisting my foot right off the end of my leg. When he'd given me the once over he let my foot drop with no warning and it banged off a table leg. I screamed and lay flat on my back making futile fists to fight the jolt of pain.

"Gotta get that shoe off," he said.

"Aren't you gonna give me something for the pain?"

"Don't got an anesthesiologist. You didn't bring nothing?"

I guessed his usual clientele either came in high on something or carried their own stash of mind numbing, muscle relaxing goodies. I had nothing. "No, I didn't. I wasn't planning on getting shot today." Though really it was a miracle I made it as long as I did.

We both turned to Skeeter who was standing in the doorway packing his glass pipe with new rocks. He caught our combined stare. "What?"

"Get over here and dose him," Mr. Gene said.

At the same time, Skeeter and I both said, "What?"

"It's gonna hurt like hell and he don't seem to want it to, so come on over here and dose him up with some of that."

"No. No way," I said.

"Will it shut him the fuck up?" Skeeter asked.

"That will or the pain will."

"Okay then."

Mr. Gene was strong for his age. He flopped his body over mine and it was like a lead blanket had fallen over my shoulders. Skeeter dug an elbow into my arm to hold it down as he leaned over, sparked the lighter and worked up a good cloud of smoke inside the bulb, then blew it into my face. I coughed and tried to turn my head, but Mr. Gene reached down and tweaked my foot so I opened my mouth wide in a shriek of pain. Skeeter blew another cloud down my throat.

Skeeter and I were getting high at about the same rate, and Mr. Gene being so close, was probably feeling pretty good himself. Exactly the kind of guy I want operating on my foot. I kicked and thrashed as much as I could but I was weak from blood loss, tired as hell and the drugs were going straight to the base of my skull and one by one turning out all the lights and replacing them with strobes and roman candles.

I was in for a wild ride, but goddammit if I didn't forget about my foot.

60
SKEETER

Once the shitheel was out and Mr. Gene was picking through the bottom of his foot, which looked like a squashed grape, I skipped out to the porch to make my call.

I admit I sparked up too soon after the first hit. And I chugged at it extra hard trying to get Brent to go loopy so I was a little out of it when I called Corgan, but he needed to hear me out.

"I should be there to close the deal," I said.

"Who the fuck is this?"

"Skeeter," I said, a little hurt he didn't know me by sound of voice.

He paused. "And why should you be there?"

"Because this is my transport. And I always finish the job, do I not?"

"Not this time."

"Unforseen circumstances. It's those two jerk-offs who gave out the wrong car. I'm the one who found the fat fuck, ain't I?"

"Aren't you the one who lost him too?"

I sputtered and spat. How could he not see my side of it? "Mr. Corgan, you gotta let me prove it to you that I can finish what I started. And whatever else you need done while I'm there, I'll finish that too."

"What are you offering exactly?"

"Like the fat fuck. He needs to go, right? Him and his fat fuck wife? And the rental guys. Them too."

He paused again, thinking it over, I bet. "You want to take them all out? You'd do that for me?"

"Sure I will. I'm more than just a delivery boy, y'know."

Corgan put a hand over the phone and spoke to someone on his end for a minute. He came back with, "Jimmy will give you the address. I'm sending two guys with Clyde. They'll have instructions. You don't do anything until they say so, undertand?"

"Yeah. Got it."

"None of this Bruce Willis shit like last time, right?"

"Sure, sure. I want to bring the stuff to you though. That's the job you hired me to do, I want to finish it."

"Anybody bringing my merchandise to me is welcome in my house any time."

"Thanks, Mr. Corgan. Thanks a lot. You won't be—"

He'd passed off the phone to Jimmy who started reading off the address before I was ready. Either way, I'd scored my ticket to the dance.

61
CLYDE

I stared at the ceiling through the slits my swollen eyelids allowed. I couldn't get enough air in my lungs and I could feel myself drifting.

"Get him up," Corgan said, and I was dragged to my feet. One of the guys had the baby in the backseat of the car. It was hot and stuffy in the warehouse and he had turned the car on and the air too. Her cries had subsided and I could see his lips moving through the window. It looked like he was trying to soothe her.

Corgan opened his mouth and started to say something, but his phone rang. He asked who the fuck it was and then listened, his eyes sliding to me in a way that made my skin crawl. "You'd do that for me?" he said and a slow smile spread across his face. He handed the phone to one of the other guys who rattled off an address. Then he took the phone and made another call. To Griffin. He said they'd meet on Colonial Parkway between Yorktown and Williamsburg. I thought about that. Colonial Parkway wound along the York River. There were pull offs where people could park their cars and fish from bridges. That could be a plus or a minus. The road was surrounded by swampy tributaries of the York River and by forest. Again, a plus or minus depending on whether I was hiding, running, or begging for my life. The only advantage I could see to the meeting place was that it was summer and Colonial Parkway was heavily traveled by tour buses. If I could get my hands on my daughter and flag someone down, I might get out of this alive.

Corgan snapped his fingers at the man in the car, who climbed out and placed my daughter in my arms. I looked at her tiny face. She was sleeping. I wondered how air could move in and out of such a tiny nose. She was beautiful. I started to cry.

Corgan handed me my phone. "Dial your wife's number," he said.

I cradled the baby with one hand and pushed the speed dial number for Madeline with the other. Corgan took the phone from me.

"Mrs. McDowd," he said. "I just wanted to let you know that your husband and daughter are safe. For now."

I could hear the ragged sound of Madeline's crying, the sound thin and brittle and like hell. She yelled, cried out. A man's voice came on and calmly asked where Corgan was, if he'd like to turn himself in. I thought of the FBI agent and the I.D. badge that I'd lost somewhere along the road. Corgan looked at me again, his eyes narrowing. His face turned red.

He clicked the phone off and removed the battery before handing it back to me.

"Let's go," he said to us all. "Time to head north toward Williamsburg."

62
LINDA

My mom sat across the table from me and lit up a cigarette. I hadn't lived with them in a few years and wasn't exactly used to the smell anymore. It was worse than Sean smelled after he'd been out mowing the lawn. It gave me a headache. On top of the throbbing in my side it made for a hell of a bad morning. No one had gotten any sleep, not really. And I know Sean thought he'd really rocked my world with the sex at the rest area. But, shit, really? No. Not at all. He calls me fat. I'm not. I'm big-boned. You try squeezing out two kids and see if you don't have a few extra pounds on you. Dumb-ass dickhead.

Mom had already slurped two cups of coffee down and was on a third. "I called Cousin Judy," she said.

Now Judy...she's fat. Makes me look like Katy Perry, tits and all.

I got up to pour myself a cup of coffee. My side was killing me and all Mom and Dad had around was ibuprofen. And now I was getting my own coffee. Jesus Christ. "Why?"

"To watch Chad and Becky while we go after Sean and Ernie."

I sat down and stared at her, taking my time drinking half the cup of coffee before I spoke again. She watched me. Mom was real good at watching. "Why? Mom, I don't think you understand what these people can do. I got shot for Christ sakes."

She moved her lips into a wrinkly pucker. I always called it the pucker of doom when I was growing up. If she was making it for Dad now, he must be in real trouble. "Which is exactly why we need to go." She pushed her coffee cup aside.

I followed her to the den where she pulled Dad's colonial rifle off the wall. It was a real colonial rifle, the kind with a bayonet. The kind you have to pack with a lead ball bullet. Dad kept this little bull's horn hanging beside it that held gun powder. A leather pouch held the packing. Dad was big into the colonial reenactments.

"He has other guns downstairs," I reminded her.

She nodded and slung the rifle over her shoulder. "I know. But this will piss him off more."

The doorbell rang and Judy walked on in. "I'm here," she called. "Where are the kids?"

"Still sleeping," Mom told her. "They eat and sleep and that's about it." Like they were five years old.

"They baked cookies," I said.

I followed mom out to her car, leaving Judy to fend for herself. "How are we going to find them, Mom?"

She pulled out her phone. "I got that app that keeps track of his whereabouts."

"Geez, Mom. That's awful."

She shrugged. "Bastard wants to mess around with a bimbo from the donut shop, then I guess I'll follow him." When I raised my eyebrows, she went on. "He had a little fling last year."

I wanted to laugh. Couldn't imagine my dad flinging with anyone. And I sure as hell couldn't imagine Mom caring about it.

But I followed her out to the car and put the colonial rifle and the lead bullets in the back seat.

63
CLYDE

My baby stayed with Corgan. I knew now with certainty that my marriage was over. There was no way Madeline would forgive this. There was no way I could even face her after all that had happened in the last twenty-four hours. Corgan had stuffed me into the back seat of a car with two thugs in the front. We were on our way to the meet.

My eyes burned and I knew I was going to cry. I tried to hold it in, but all I succeeded in doing was making snorting sounds and blowing snot out of my nose.

"What the fuck, dude?" one of the thugs said.

I buried my face in my hands and just cried. Bawled like a fucking baby. The driver muttered something under his breath. I just kept my face in my hands and howled.

"Holy fuck," the other one said and I could feel the car swerving and making a sharp right turn.

One of them smacked me on the top of the head. "Jesus Christ, pull it together, dude."

"Go get him a bottle of water or something. People are going to wonder what the shit is going on."

"Fuck." The passenger door opened and closed and I was alone with the driver.

If I had been in a movie, it would have been the part where I made a break for it and saved my baby girl. But it wasn't a movie. Corgan had my kid. All I could do was cry about it.

64
SEAN

Detroit, for most of its existence, has been the murder capital of America. New York had it's heyday in the seventies, but Detroit came back strong and hasn't relinquished the title since. Still, in all my years I never so much as saw a gun in someone's hand. Now, in one long weekend in Virginia I feel like I'm in the middle of a rap music video.

I stood outside in a tiny parking lot just off the Parkway. I could see a bridge and had a feeling I might get the call to go over there and make the switch in the middle of the span or something. That felt like something a drug dealer would do. I guess so, anyway.

My jacket was making me sweat, but I run a little hot anyway. A few extra pounds will do that to you. I guess I carry more than a few. But no way was I going to take off the jacket. It was hiding the pistol in my waistband.

Ernie insisted on hiding in the trees. He'd brought some high powered scope for his rifle and he claimed, with nothing to back it up as usual, that he could hit a guy through the pupil of one eye from three hundred yards or some ridiculous shit like that. He kept saying he would "cover" me. So why did I feel so uncovered?

The suitcase at my feet held the drugs. It felt weird, emptying out my suitcase of clothes and toothpaste and filling it full of plastic wrapped narcotics. It felt almost as weird as packing up the bundles of cash from the office the day before I split town with the money that was owed me. Both times I packed a suitcase with something that could get me arrested. Easy money. Dear God, there's no such thing, is there? That idea is the Bigfoot of the criminal set. They want to believe it, many spend a lifetime pursuing it. But when the facts are laid out, the bastard just doesn't exist.

Not in Virginia anyway.

65
CLYDE

I breathed a sigh of relief when I saw the fat man, Griffin, waiting in the lot. I'd regained control of my emotions enough that I wouldn't be an embarrassment, but really I was an observer in this whole deal. It felt like I was watching an auction on my daughter's life. If things went my way, she lived. If other people fucked it up, I would lose it all.

The tears threatened to come back.

The driver parked and waited. He and his pal scoped out the area. I saw three cars near the edges of the lot, all by a foot path which led down to the river. For fishing, probably. Enjoying a day on the river as a family. Lucky fucks.

There was no traffic on the bridge. Nobody milling around. Nothing to stop this deal.

"Let's go," I said.

They ignored me and finished their sweep of the area at their own pace. In synchronous motion their doors opened at the same time.

"Okay," the driver said. "Let's do this."

I got out and stayed behind them. Griffin looked nervous. I could see him sweat and he swayed a little on his feet. What the hell did he have to be nervous about? His fucking kids weren't in the balance.

The driver pointed to the suitcase at Griffin's feet. "That for me?"

Griffin started to speak, but his mouth was dry. He swallowed. "Money first," he said.

My two companions shared a look like, "This guy, right?" I knew the truth. They never intended to pay him. Why would they? Corgan couldn't let some tourist come in and screw up his day and then let him walk away. It sent the wrong message, and as I learned all too well, Corgan's messages were hard to misinterpret.

The driver spoke again, his partner always scanning the horizon for trouble. "Why don't we cut the bullshit and do this like professionals?"

"I am," Griffin said. "Money first, then the case." His words were hard, but his attitude said pure jelly.

"Gene." The partner nodded his head and the driver followed his gaze. A beat up Honda was pulling into the lot. It banged over the entry and headed for our group. It took me a moment, but as it got closer I could see the driver.

"Shit," I said. Somewhere far away, I swore I could hear my little girl crying.

66
SKEETER

Fuckers started my meet up without me.

Brent was in the seat next to me still bugging out. He kept chattering but not saying real words, like he was speed reading a long list of things written with no spaces or nothing. Man, I wish crystal still got me that high.

I put it in park and left her running. "Y'all save any cake for me?" I said as I walked toward the group of assholes in front of me. Corgan's two goons I recognized. Gene and the other one, Tricky. And Clyde. Pussy looked like a bitch on her period, all red eyes and snotty nose. Then the fat man. He didn't like the look of me, that's for sure.

"What?" Gene said.

"Well, y'all started the party without me. Did you save me a slice of cake?"

I didn't wait for no invitation. I walked right across the divide between them, a wide berth you could have driven a Peterbilt through. I got right up close to Griffin and put a hand on the suitcase.

"Mr. Corgan thanks you, and I thank you." I lifted the case. Good 'n heavy. "You fat fuck," I said. Then I spun on my heel and stared walkin' back to my car. Yessir, Corgan was going to get his load and I was going to get my promotion.

"The fuck you doin' Skeeter?" Gene said.

"What? I came to get my delivery. That's what the fuck I'm doin'"

Clyde found his voice all of sudden. "Skeeter, stop. Corgan sent us to get that."

"Wrong, boyo. He sent me to get it yesterday morning. You fucked that up. I'm just doin' what I said I'd do when I took the job. See, I believe in my work and my word. If you don't, well, that's between you and the good Lord." I laughed out loud.

"And Corgan, who just might send you to see the Man upstairs real soon. Fuckin' know I would."

I reached my car. Gene and Tricky were walking my way now. "Skeeter, he sent us down here special to get that case."

"Then you should have took it. Look at y'all, standing around with your dicks in your hands like you're afraid of this motherfucker. Look at him." I threw an arm out to Griffin so we could all gander at his disgusting disgustingness. "He's fat, he's scared and he ain't armed."

Imagine my surprise when a bullet ripped into the suitcase.

67
SEAN

I knew Ernie couldn't take anybody's eye out. But I didn't know if that's what he was aiming for. But with that one shot, boy, things got real ugly.

"Everybody hold the fuck still," Ernie called as he stepped out from behind a tree. He kept one eye behind his scope and moved out of cover of one tree and stepped artfully behind another.

"Jesus Christ," the skinny dope fiend said. He held up the suitcase and examined the hole in it. Then he dropped it and dropped to his knees at the same time. He did one of those weird Hollywood-style shoulder rolls in the dust and came up behind the trunk of his car. He squeezed off two rounds: pop, pop! At the two guys in suits. They fell, motionless, in the tall grass.

"Holy shit!" the guy in scrubs, Clyde, said, ducking beside the Tahoe he'd arrived in. "Holy shit. I just want my kid. I just want my kid."

"Okay, fuckers," the druggie said. "Just you and me now. Corgan's gonna be pissed you killed his two favorite bitches."

The little shit was going to blame us. I squeezed off a round, aiming for his tires so he couldn't get away. The guy deserved a bullet between the eyes, but I didn't have the stomach for killing someone. And my aim was horrible. Dust kicked up in front of the driver's side front tire.

Someone yelled "Don't shoot!" A woman's voice. I looked up and saw Betty and Linda climbing up the bank toward the end of the bridge.

"Jesus goddamn Christ, Betty," Ernie yelled. "Get down. Are you crazy?"

"Yeah I'm crazy," she said, out of breath, "and you're an asshole."

Linda struggled up behind her, clutching her side.

"He's got a gun," Ernie yelled. "Stay down for chrissakes."

Linda pulled a gun I recognized from Ernie's gun rack and shot it into the air. It went off with a blast like a cannon and a puff of black smoke.

The skinny druggie fired a round in their direction and Ernie shot at him. I ducked and shot too, although I don't know what I was aiming at.

Clyde covered his ears and duck-walked around the back of the Tahoe. He was crying.

The drug guy opened the passenger door of the car he was driving and pulled a man from the front seat. It was Brent from the rental shop. His foot was wrapped in a bloody bandage. He looked like he'd been through a blender. Drug guy held Brent up in front of him, like a human shield.

"Who the hell is that?," Ernie called to me.

"Which one?"

"The one with the bloody foot?"

Drug guy squeezed off a shot and it kicked off some tree bark in front of Ernie.

"Son of a bitch," Ernie yelled.

"The guy with the foot is from the rental place. Rented me the car."

"Good or bad? Good or bad?"

I shook my head to clear it. "Uh. Good. I think." He was singing something and spit bubbles frothed at his lips. He was clearly stoned out of his mind. Drug guy squeezed off another shot and just like that, my leg was on fire. It buckled under me.

"Goddamn son of a bitch," Ernie yelled. Linda and Betty poked their heads over the edge of the bridge.

"Hurts, doesn't it?" Linda yelled. Bitch.

Drug guy tossed Brent to the ground and climbed back into his car. His tires squealed as he pulled away.

68
CLYDE

I tried to catch my breath. My nose was swollen from crying again. Not my manliest moment. I was tired of it. Tired of being scared, tired of feeling helpless. My kid was in danger. My baby girl.

An old man stepped out from the woods. "Goddamn, son, stop your whining." For a minute I thought he was talking to me, but then I noticed that the fat guy was on the ground, clutching his leg. "I got shot up worse than that in 'Nam, and I didn't make a peep. Now get up and shut up."

The old man strolled over to me. "Now who the hell are you, son?"

"I'm Clyde." At least that's what I think I said. I was watching as two women crossed the bridge and joined us on the other side in the pull off. "They have my baby."

"Ernie, are those men dead?" Two women had crossed the bridge and stood now with us in the pull off.

"Son of a bitch, Betty. I told you to stay at home. And you," he glared at the woman with her. "What the hell are you doing with my rifle? Son of a goddamn bitch."

"Sean, are you okay?" The younger of the two women knelt beside the man on the ground. "I told you it hurts." She pulled a cloth out of the enormous bag she had slung over her shoulder and pressed it to his lower leg, where blood dripped at a sluggish rate onto the dust.

"You're Griffin?" I asked the old man.

He shook his head and nodded at the fat guy on the ground. "That's him. I'm just along for the ride. And you..." he spoke to the older woman, grabbing her by the elbow and dragging her out of ear shot.

"You fucking asshole," I said, kicking the guy in the gut. "You fucking, fucking asshole."

"Fucking asshole," Brent was there, on the ground, his foot

wrapped in a bloody rag. He giggled. "Griffin is a fucking asshole."

I ran a hand over my face. It was hot and getting hotter. And there were two bodies on the ground. A bus rattled over the bridge and curious tourists peered from the windows. They seemed to be more focused on Brent's bloody foot and the bloody fat guy on the ground. But the bus was speeding up as it crossed the bridge and I knew there were probably all sorts of people on board punching 911 into their cell phones.

"That's it, time to go," the old man said.

I picked up the brief case with the drugs inside. In his hurry to leave, Skeeter dropped it on the ground. He would no doubt be back.

I looked at the car I had arrived in, started toward it.

"Nope. Not that one," he said. He gestured to the Tahoe. "Climb in. Everyone in."

"We brought the minivan," the old woman said.

"Goddamn it, Betty. Where is it?"

"Down the road a ways. In the trees."

"Get it. Meet us back home."

"Oh no. I'm coming with you. I'll follow you into Williamsburg. We can leave the van in a lot there."

I could see the wheels turning in the old man's head. He didn't want her to tag along, but she likely had him over a barrel. Women were like that. Trouble makers.

He gestured to me. "You. Bring that here."

I stood where I was. He could shoot me. He could leave me out here for the fish to eat. But he wasn't going to get the briefcase without a fight.

"Fuck you," I said.

Mrs. Griffin helped her husband into the Tahoe. She looked annoyed for a minute, but the pair exchanged a small smile as she closed the back door. I moved toward the sedan again.

"Son," the old guy said to me. "Seems to me that young drug addict is going to be coming back for what's in that briefcase. Maybe you won't want to be in possession of it when that happens. How's about you give it to me?"

"They've got my kid. My daughter."

"It's a girl," Brent said from the ground. "Congrats, man. I'm happy for you. Seriously, man, that's really great."

The women stared at me for a minute and then disappeared down the bank and across the marsh toward where they had hidden their car.

The old man's face fell for a minute and he appeared to be thinking. I eyed the sedan and wondered if the driver had left the keys in the ignition or if they were in his pocket. I didn't want to turn a dead guy over and search him. "Well then," he said after a minute. "Let's go get your baby."

I didn't trust him. Why should I? But we were running out of time. The people on the bus had seen us. There wasn't much else to do. We had to get moving. Fast. I picked Brent up off the ground and helped him into the Tahoe.

It was ten minutes to Old Town Williamsburg. We stashed the minivan in a public lot behind a church and the women climbed into the car.

"This is so exciting," the old lady said. "Let's all introduce ourselves."

69
SKEETER

Okayokayokayokayoayokay. Stories straight time. These two big fuckers come out of the woods, blast the two drivers, try to kill me, so I bailed. Live to fight another day, otherwise we'll never get your stash back, Mr. Corgan.

The whole goddamn thing must have been a set up organized by Clyde. He must have hired the fat man to take the Tahoe in the first place. This whole crazy shitbag of a mess has been a double cross from the start. More than likely.

Well, no mind, no mind. We still got what matters to Clyde. We still got chips in the game. And it's win-win for me when Corgan sees that the same psycho fucks who killed two of his best guys couldn't kill me 'cause I'm like a motherfucking cockroach, and I don't mind sayin' it. I admire the lowly cockroach. Sucker's been around for millions of years and can survive the nuclear apocalypse? That is bad-ass, man. Wish that nickname had stuck before Skeeter. I'd be proud to be called Roach.

But, shit, I dunno. Maybe this is my cue. Maybe this is where I get off this crazy train and pull up stakes for green pastures. Someplace I can start over, get in with a new crew. Someone who treats me with some goddamn respect. Someone who calls me Roach.

70
BRENT

The face that came into focus wasn't what I expected. She had to be in her seventies. How the hell did she get to be a part of this?

We were all crammed in the Tahoe like we were on vacation or something, Clyde and I in the third row of seats like were kids stuffed in the way back.

My brain started to come out of the cotton candy it'd been covered in for the past hour. With it came my foot pain, but I was okay with it now. I heard the old guy in the front talking with...was it Griffin? Jesus, it was. We're in Griffin's car, which meant this was our car. Our rental. The stupid car that started all this shit. I looked over Griffin's head and saw the loose seam in the ceiling fabric.

They were discussing some sort of plan.

"I can get us in," Clyde said. Christ, he looked shell shocked. Real PTSD stuff on his face. I saw that look from a buddy of mine when he got back from Afghanistan.

"Then it'll be you and me," the old man said. Who was the old man? "You can get us there?" he asked Clyde.

"It's programmed in the GPS. This was the car that was supposed to bring the load in the first place."

Griffin, in the passenger seat, punched the screen with his fat fingers and smeared blood on the GPS unit. Was everyone in here shot?

Before long I heard that robot woman's voice telling us to keep on the highway for another thirty-five miles. I had a little while at least so I closed my eyes and tried to scrape off more of the cotton candy.

71
CLYDE

We pulled the Tahoe to a stop in front of Corgan's house. A few days late, but we finally made it. I had the package. I hoped he had my daughter. I hoped she wouldn't remember any of this, even deep down in her subconscious.

The old guy, Ernie, really seemed to be taking a leadership role, but now that we were here, it was my turn to deal with the top man. Ernie, however, insisted on coming with me.

"You don't just walk in there alone and hand over his goods," he said. "You need someone with you to show a little muscle. That's what these guys know. It's their language."

I didn't really want to know how exactly this old man knew what language an animal like Corgan spoke, but I wanted to get things moving to so I didn't argue.

"Whatever, let's just go."

Ernie had more instructions. "Sean, you take the ladies and the rifle and stake out the bushes. I want you far enough away from any trouble, yet close enough to lend a hand if we need it."

"Okay, I guess. But shouldn't we—"

Ernie cut him off with a stare and a stern, "Do it."

His wife kissed him on the cheek as she got out with her wounded daughter and wounded son-in-law. I knew they'd be no help at all and suspected Ernie was just putting them out of the way with a fake sense that they had a job to do. Fine by me.

"You," he said to Brent. "Get behind the wheel. Be ready to drive. Are you good? Your head clear?"

Brent said, "Yes," but he sounded a little hung over. He shook out his face, slapped his cheeks and came around. "I'm good," he said.

I put out a hand and he shook it. "I owe you one, bro. For all this."

"I'd say you owe me my job back, but I don't want a goddamn thing to do with cars for a long time."

"I hear you."

I pressed the briefcase to my chest. The bullet hole in it stared out like an eye. Ragged, beaten and worse for the wear, I took Corgan's dope delivery to his front door.

When the bell rang I heard a dog bark and my daughter cry. My hand went for the knob, but I stopped myself. I saw Ernie next to me giving me a hard look. The old man held a pistol in his hand.

"You gonna stash that thing?" I asked him.

"You ever been to an orgy, son?"

I scrunched my face at him. "No."

"You show up some place and you know there's a decent chance you're gonna get fucked, best for you to walk in showing everyone what you're packing."

I bet this guy had been toting that analogy around since Vietnam.

The door opened. One of Corgan's henchmen stood there looking beefy and mountainous. He gave us a silent look, noticed the gun in Ernie's hand down by his hip. He stared back at the old man and they had a little contest. Ernie didn't blink.

"Come on, man," I said. "I got the stuff, let's get going. Where's my daughter?"

The guy stepped clear of the doorway. I moved to go inside but Ernie put a hand on my arm. "We'll wait here."

"What? No. I want to see my daughter."

"Tell him to bring her here. We do the trade and we leave. Simple as that."

The henchman smiled at the brass balls on Ernie. I felt like he was making a huge mistake. When the henchman turned and walked back into the house I turned to Ernie.

"You don't want to piss this guy off. Haven't you been paying attention to anything in the past twenty-four hours?"

"There's no reason we need to go inside. He's got the advantage in there. Just settle the fuck down."

He cracked his neck and rolled his shoulders. This guy had some sort of history and I'm sure I didn't want to know it.

Corgan approached the door with an extra henchman to make bookends around him.

"Mr. McDowd," he said. "Better late than never, right?" He smiled and pointed to the case I was still hugging to my chest.

"I hope you know this was all beyond my control, Mr. Corgan." I held out the case and one of the guys next to him reached out to take it. Once again, Ernie's hand came up to stop us. Only by gently resting a palm on the other man's hand did the entire transaction come to a halt.

"First the girl," he said. Jesus H. Christ I would kill him if he fucked this up for me.

Corgan studied Ernie intently. "I don't think we've had the pleasure."

"We're not here for pleasure. We're here for the child. You see what you want, let's see what we want and then we can all be on our way."

Corgan smiled and gave a miniscule nod. His right hand man lowered his hand away from the case. I was left holding it out at the end of my tired-growing arms.

"That's the thing about the older generation. No time for bullshit, am I right?"

Ernie gave him a stone-faced nod. Corgan snapped his fingers and the crying sounds got louder as a beefy man dressed all in black brought my infant daughter to the doorway. Instantly tears rained from my eyes. I thrust the case out farther, both for them to take it and be done with this and to free up my hands to be able to hold her.

"Okay," Corgan said. "I'm sorry it had to come to this, Clyde. Children should never be involved."

I was too choked up to agree with him. The same henchman reached for the case again. Ernie stayed put this time but a rifle shot rang out from behind us in the yard. It smacked the side of the house somewhere up near the second floor. Corgan took a step back into the house, his two guards flanking him both had pistols in their hands before I could blink. The man holding my daughter pulled her closer to his chest which made her cries intensify.

Corgan stepped up and put a gun to my child's head.

"No," I called. I knew I'd never be able to burn the image from my memory.

"The fuck is this, McDowd?" Corgan said.

Ernie held out a hand, keeping his gun low and pointed at the ground. "Calm down. That was nothing. If I'm correct, it's my dumb-as-shit son-in-law making a really stupid fucking mistake."

We all held out breath while we waited to see if Corgan bought it.

"Sorry about that," came Griffin's voice from the far reaches of the yard. "My bad. Gun just went off."

Ernie's wife shouted in a scolding tone. "I told him I could hold the damn gun."

"See there?" Ernie said. "Just one dumb-ass doing what he does best. Sooner we do this swap, sooner we leave and take all dumbasses with us."

I could only focus on a tiny window in my view where the barrel of Corgan's gun touched my daughter's bright pink head. Nothing ever looked so ugly. "Please," I whispered.

Corgan looked from me to Ernie, past us into the yard. Satisfied that no other shots were coming, he put the gun down. "Give him the kid."

The case was snatched out of my hand and replaced with my daughter. She felt so soft and so light. I pulled her close, kissing the spot on her head where a tiny ring of redness had risen from the barrel of Corgan's gun.

"That's that," Ernie said. "Good day to you." He tugged at my arm and I followed him back to the SUV, never taking my eyes off my little girl.

72
BRENT

It was kinda convenient that we had to go to the hospital for Clyde since me and both Griffins needed a doctor anyway. One stop shopping.

I felt like shit and driving was hard. About half way there I had to pull over and let Ernie take over. I went back to the third row seat and tried to shut my eyes. Clyde's little girl kept crying off and on, but he did a pretty good job of keeping her calm and quiet. I watched him and he never took his eyes off her for a second.

We were far from scot-free, but we escaped with our lives, which is more than I thought I'd get out of this. We looked like we'd just come off the front lines—all shot up, bleeding, exhausted. There would be questions at the ER. Ernie started running down our stories. Hunting accidents, all of them. As long as we all stood by our stories and didn't press charges on anyone, what could the cops do? It's not illegal to get shot, only to do the shooting.

As ragged as we all were, that tiny pink bundle was like a shining star in our midst. As badly as we had all fucked up in this past week, maybe in our whole lives that led us here, that little kid was hope in a blanket. Unsullied, untarnished. She'd never have any idea she spent her first day of life so close to death.

I looked at that bundle in Clyde's arms and I knew we'd be okay.

73
CLYDE

Agent Stu Trumble glared at me as I walked into the maternity ward with my baby girl. I was vaguely aware of police officers reaching for her, wanting the nursing staff to check her out. Ernie was there to keep them at bay.

Trumble knew nothing about the drugs, nothing about what I had been doing the last few days. As far as he was concerned, this was a kidnapping, plain and simple. Someone had targeted my shop, when I wasn't there. They went after my family. It was a strange situation, but they must have seen stranger. For now, I had just solved his case, had just brought back my own daughter, had rescued the victim. Sure there would be questions, but I would field them when they came in. I didn't know how yet, but I'd do it.

Madeline was up and dressed in sweats and a baggy shirt. She looked beautiful. She burst into tears when she saw me. I placed our daughter in her arms. She stared at our baby for a few minutes and then she looked up and noticed Brent and the Griffin family.

She nodded once at Brent, then looked the Griffins over from head to toe. "Who the hell are all these people?"

Trumble was there too and didn't give me a chance to answer. "I guess you'll need to answer some questions," he said, his hand on my arm. Keep calm and act dumb, I thought. Keep calm and act dumb.

Madeline met my eyes. She was still trying to make sense of the crowd of people I'd brought with me: Brent with his bloody foot, Sean with his bullet wound to the gut, me in scrubs with two black eyes, a fat lady, and an old couple. She was angry and bewildered and I couldn't tell if she was willing to listen to anything I had to say.

"You can't all be in here." It was the angry nurse. Her opinion of me hadn't changed much in the last day.

I looked at Trumble. "I'll come with you. Some of these folks need attention."

"Then they can go to the emergency room like all the other patients with acute injuries," the nurse said. "Honestly."

I didn't have the chance to see where everyone went. Trumble had me by the arm and steered me down the hallway toward an empty room.

74
SEAN

"Shot himself hunting," Ernie said to the ER doctor. I hoped to hell they didn't ask me what we were hunting because I had no clue. I'd never been hunting a day in my life, and I had no idea what season it was. Summer. What the hell did people hunt in summer? Not deer. Not duck. I thought hunting was only in the fall.

"I'd be careful who you tell that to," the doctor said. He looked like he was twelve years old. "You could get a ticket for hunting out of season."

The ER was busy, but then what ER wasn't busy? They put that Brent guy in a regular room. He was going to need surgery on his foot, but they wouldn't do that until morning. I wasn't hurt bad, so they patched me up and let me go. I needed to see the Brent kid, to at least tell him no hard feelings. Somehow things got a lot more messed up than I had planned on and I couldn't stand the thought of him getting hurt on account of me. I just wanted to make some extra money.

Ernie pulled a chair up beside the bed and gave me a hard look. "What the hell, son? This was about the most fucked up twenty-four hours I've ever spent."

I opened my mouth to answer. I don't remember what it was that I was going to say, probably something about wanting to make it all right again, planning to return the money I had stolen, planning to be a better husband to Linda. Who the hell knows?

"Don't say anything now," he said. "But think about what you want to do with your life. Think about your wife and kids. Think about not being a total fuck up."

I'd had enough. Not even twelve hours earlier, he told me he wanted me out of Linda's life. "You're the one who wanted to take them for more money," I said.

Ernie sat back in the chair and chewed on his lip for a bit.

Then he stood up and said he was going to go find the ladies. As soon as he left I stood up and put my shirt on and headed out to find Brent's room.

75
CLYDE

Trumble didn't keep me long. Just asked me a bunch of stuff about the type of car the kidnapper drove, the places we went, how I knew to follow him. I gave him everything I had on Skeeter. Guy kept hanging around my car lot. Kept threatening my staff. Bashed through the front window. Came here and took my kid. Maybe it was some sort of obsession. Maybe not. He said he had enough information for now. So he let me go but told me not to leave town. Fine by me. I needed to see Brent for a few minutes and then I wanted to be with Madeline and our daughter.

Sean Griffin was already in with Brent by the time I got to the room. Brent was pretty out of it. They had given him one of those medication pumps where he could dose himself whenever he had pain. He seemed pretty happy to see me.

"How's it going?" he said, smiling. "You look like shit."

I rubbed a hand over my chin. "Yeah," I said. "Madeline is pretty pissed."

"What about the cops?"

I shrugged. "They still think this is just a kidnapping. Looking for the guys. We gave them some bogus information about cars and a stalker who was after my agency. Some skinny guy with tattoos."

He smiled at that. "Skeeter," he said.

"We'll see if they buy it. I wouldn't lay money on it though."

I was hoping Skeeter was dead in a ditch someplace and when they found his body that would be it, case closed. Everything would go back to normal and I could get on with my life with Madeline and our baby girl.

Sean Griffin moved a little slowly, but he made it a point to move over and stand in front of me.

"I want to say I'm sorry. For everything," he said. "I don't know what got into me."

I wanted to punch him in the face, rip his throat out, but the truth is, I was just too fucking tired. "Fine." was all I said.

We heard the footsteps first, the clicking of hard soles on tile, the whistling of a tuneless song, and then he was there. Skeeter. Standing in the doorway. A nurse had shown him the way. He had linked a police badge around his neck and looked like some sort of New York back-street detective, bad teeth and all. He smiled at her and although she cringed a little when he laid his eyes on her, she gave him a nod. "Just don't stay too long," she said, backing out. "The patient needs his rest." She closed the door as she left and Skeeter regarded us with narrowed, bloodshot eyes.

"Well, well, well, this here's a classy fuck-you, how do you do, ain't it?"

Brent shrank into the bed, his face as white as the sheet. I moved to stand so he couldn't see Skeeter and Skeeter couldn't see him.

"It's over, Skeeter. They've got the stuff they wanted, we got my kid back. You're out of line here."

"The fuck you know about being out of line?" he asked. He moved his hand to his hip and that's when I noticed the gun he had there. I didn't know anything about guns. Glock? Nine millimeter? Thirty-eight special? Meant nothing to me. "You screwed me good, Clyde-mother-fucking-McDowd. How's about you pay me for my trouble?"

"You want cash you're going to have to take it up with Corgan."

"Fuck that," he said.

Sean held his hands out. "This place is crawling with cops, Skeeter. You don't want to do anything stupid."

Skeeter drew the gun. "I want any shit out of you, tubby, I'll squeeze your head."

"I'll push my call button and bring the nurse in here." Brent's voice trembled as he spoke, but I could tell he meant what he said.

"Try it," Skeeter said, drawing the gun and pointing it at my chest.

"Easy there, fella." Sean moved to stand between me and Skeeter. "I've got some money. Some cash I stashed away before

I left Detroit. It's right around forty-five K at this point in time. Will that be enough?"

"Look, Griffin," I said.

"Shut the fuck up, Clyde," Skeeter hissed.

"Just come with me," Sean said. "Come with me and leave these fellas alone. They've been through enough."

Skeeter holstered his gun. "Lead on."

I followed them from the room. Skeeter made a big production of informing the nurses he was taking Sean into custody. I had no idea where they were going, but I knew I needed to tell his family he'd been taken. I hurried off to find Ernie.

76
SEAN

At least this damn money will be good for something. I had to reach back to the top of my long list of regrets to get to the cash I'd embezzled. Good God, I was an embezzler. I'd been so filled with righteous indignation that I never saw it like that. I guess I had some sort of Robin Hood complex about it.

Well, now the money wasn't going to the good guys at all. It was going to him. A man named Skeeter.

Maybe. I got him out of the hospital, that was step one. Step two I hadn't thought of yet. I needed to stall the little creep. Come to think of it, Skeeter was a perfect name for the annoying shit. If only I could swat him away.

"So where are we going, pops?"

He kept a hand on my elbow like he was removing me under police escort. Nobody bothered to ask where his handcuffs were. And how anyone ever thought this scruffy looking punk was a cop, I'll never know. They must have thought he was some undercover guy or something.

"I can't get it right away," I said.

He stopped us. "Okay, what is this shit. You just told me—"

"I can get it for you. Just not right this second. I don't have it on me. I've been a little preoccupied lately, you know what I mean?"

"How long?"

"I'm not sure."

He threw his hands up and let them come slapping back down to his legs like a spoiled child not getting what he wants. I knew that move well from my own kids. Shit, my kids. I'd almost forgotten about them. That's not good.

"Well, what the shit do we do until you can get it?" he asked.

"I ain't just sittin' around with my thumb up my ass waiting to get caught, y'know?"

"My bank is in Detroit. Give me an account and I can wire you the money when I get back there."

"What the...?" Skeeter's hand went to his gun, but it stayed in his belt. "You think I trust you as far as I can throw you, fat man?"

"Three days, tops. I just need to get the hell out of Virginia."

Skeeter started twitching his body, shuffling his feet. He was annoyed and it worked him like electric shocks. "Nah, nah, man. This ain't gonna do. No fuckin' way. Three days? Shit." He spit out the side of his mouth. "Three days? Okay, here's what we're gonna do. You're gonna go to Detroit and get me my money and your wife, the fat lady, she's gonna stay here with me. She sticks to me like white on rice until I get paid. But you don't got to worry none on her, not like I'm gonna be raping her or nothing."

"She's in surgery for her bullet wound," I lied. "The one you gave her."

Skeeter grunted like he'd stubbed his toe. "Then you go tomorrow." He punched the air. "Fuck."

"What do we do until then?"

"You stick with me. And I need to get the fuck out of here right now and go see a friend. So come on."

He jerked at my elbow again and we started walking to the parking garage.

"Where are we going?"

"I told you I need to see a friend. I need to get good and fucking high if you want to know. This bullshit is too much. And here's a news flash fat boy—you're paying my tab."

Great. Funding a drug deal. Small potatoes on my list of offenses this trip. Probably won't even make it onto the police report. At least it gives me more time to think.

77
CLYDE

Madeline still wasn't all that interested in talking to me.

"Do you swear this is over now, Clyde?" Her bag was packed, ready to leave the hospital. She was being discharged. Our daughter was still being checked by the doctors and the cops. I didn't know what was taking so long. She was obviously fine.

"Babe," I said. "I need to go talk to one more guy. We're almost done. And yes, I swear this will be behind us soon." I needed to get Griffin back. If Skeeter got him injured or if they both got picked up, our entire story could fall apart.

"Not soon. Now." Something about her demeanor was different now. She'd toughened up. I don't know if it was the twenty-four hours without her newborn child or the act of pushing a human being through her vagina, but she was hardened. That did not bode well for me. It also made me pull one last lie out of the bag.

"Yes. Right now. Let me just go tell them that we're done and we can get out of here."

I found Ernie in the cafeteria sitting with his wife.

"We have a situation," I said.

He looked his age as he sighed and set down his coffee cup. "Again?"

"Skeeter was just here. He took Sean."

"Which one's Skeeter?"

"The skinny bastard who likes to shoot first."

The wife spoke up. "He's the one who shot Linda, Ern."

"He is, huh?" Ernie looked from his wife to me. "Took Sean, huh?"

"Yeah. He was looking for money. Sean said he had some to give. I don't know if he was just baiting him or what."

"Baiting him with what? That rat bastard doesn't have two nickels to rub together."

"Ernie," his wife said. "There's the money Linda told us about."

Ernie put a hand over his eyes. "Aw, shit, that's right. His stolen cash that started this whole mess."

"What stolen cash?" I said.

"It's a long story and it's been a long day. Maybe we can use this, though. The son of a bitch finally did something right by offering that money up to the likes of that little druggie." He kicked out a chair for me and motioned for me to sit. "Let's talk this out."

78
BRENT

I guess crutches weren't covered by my insurance. You can't even describe what I was doing as a limp, more like a hop then a skip step. Little noises kept escaping my throat because every time I set my foot down on the floor it felt like I'd stepped on a rusty nail. And the damn flap on the back of my hospital robe kept waving open and letting in a breeze. At least I kept on my shorts.

The wrapping around my foot was a bloody mess. I had a feeling I'd popped a stitch or two with this hopping around, but no way was I gonna let Clyde handle Skeeter on his own. When that little rat bastard walked out with Sean I wanted to let them go. Sean would be getting the karma he deserved for trying to hang on to the drugs in the first place. Then Clyde went after them and I knew we weren't done.

I got a few looks from orderlies and a nurse once, but no one told me to stop or brought me back to my room. Nice security. It was easy to see how Skeeter got inside in the first place. Or how Clyde's daughter got taken. We got problems with health care in this country and issue number one is that nobody seems to give a fuck.

Oh well. The lady doctor who stitched up my foot was nice. She frowned a little bit at the bargain basement surgery job done by the doc Skeeter took me to, but in the end even she admitted there wasn't much more that could be done. It just needed to heal. She put in a few extra stitches, then she shot me up with a lot of Novocaine or whatever it was. Kept talking about her three kids, one in college. Said she just got back into medicine, just moved back to the area. I wasn't much for small talk. I kinda tuned out when she started talking about her belly dancing classes. It did keep my mind off my foot for a second though.

OVER THEIR HEADS

I forced myself to quit pushing the pain killer button on my IV. Nothing would have been better than to just lay there and sleep off the last thirty-six hours, but now I had to find Clyde. I wanted in on this posse. I pulled the IV line out and pushed myself to my feet. It took a few minutes for the dizziness to pass, but when it did I moved along as fast as my broken foot would carry me.

The waiting room was empty of our little crew. I made it to the maternity ward but Clyde wasn't there either.

By the time I hopped into the cafeteria, Clyde and Ernie were wrapping up.

"So who gets to make the call?" Clyde asked.

"Better you do it," Ernie said.

I bumped a chair as I joined their table. "Howdy boys," I said, grateful to finally get off my feet. "I want in."

79
CLYDE

Sometimes I don't think I deserve a friend as good as Brent. I certainly thought it when he hobbled into the hospital cafeteria with his boxers hanging out of his hospital gown and his foot in a three-foot-thick bandage. He insisted on being a part of the plan. I started to tell him no, and then he told me to fuck off. Just like that. Then he pulled out a chair and sat down, stealing my coffee as he did. I looked at Ernie, who just shrugged. "Could use all the help we can get," he said, so we filled him in.

"It's asking a lot," Ernie said when we finished laying out the plan.

"It's gonna save his ass," I said.

"Yeah, but counting on him to play along? I don't give my son-in-law credit for much, but brains is lowest on the list. I guess after his ability to do pushups."

Brent slurped on my coffee, then said, "I'm more worried about Skeeter."

"Not me," I said. "He'll smell the money and come running."

Ernie handed over his cell phone. "Let's hope that boy doesn't fuck it up before it begins."

"Yeah," I said, taking the phone and pressing send on the number Ernie had called up for me. "Let's hope."

80
SKEETER

The fat guy's cell phone rang. We hadn't made it to S-Dogg's place yet so I hadn't scored and I was pissed about it. I should have made the fat fucker drive.

"Well, answer it you pile of shit," I said.

Took him forever to dig the thing out of his pocket. I don't know what the shit his ring tone was. Some top forty fag shit.

"Hello?" He palmed the phone. "It's Clyde."

"Well what the fuck does he want?"

"What is it Clyde?"

I slapped the side of his head with a palm. "Put it on speaker dipshit."

He did. Clyde started talkin' real fast.

"We got your money, Skeeter."

Bullshit. "Where?"

"It's at the rental shop. Griffin left behind two suitcases. His wife says the kids were supposed to bring them but they forgot." I smiled. Sounds typical. Stupid dumbshit kids. "We had them held aside waiting for them to return the vehicle. Turns out one of those suitcases had his money in it."

I looked at Griffin. "That true?"

"If my wife says it's true, then it's true. She handles the packing."

He could tell by my look that I thought this smelled like a ripe fart. "I dunno."

"And I'll tell you what, I wouldn't put it past those kids to throw one more wrench in the works like this. I swear to God almighty some days I wish I'd gotten dogs instead."

I pulled to a stop at a red light. S-Dogg was still fifteen minutes away. The airport was maybe twenty in the other direction. "Where do I find it?"

Clyde got a little giddyup in his voice. "In the back there's a lost and found for luggage and other stuff we pull out of the cars after they're checked in. It wouldn't have been wrecked in the crash. They're still in there."

I kinda wish I hadn't shot that cop now. The place might be crawling with more boys in blue ready to cock block me from my money.

"What if I can't just walk in and get it?"

"I'll get it for you," Clyde said.

"You'd do that?"

"If it means all this shit is over and I can go home with my wife and daughter, hell yes, I'd do that."

The light turned green. I stayed still. Griffin was sweating, but that was nothing new. The car behind us honked.

"Tell you what," I said. "You meet me there and—"

HONK again.

"We meet up at your car place and—"

HONK.

"Hold on a sec."

I jerked the door open and wiped my nose with the back of my hand as I took five long strides to the shitty little Jap hybrid behind us. I pulled my gun from my belt.

"I'm on the motherfucking phone and you honking your damn horn isn't helping me do the business I need to do." The driver, a shit scared dude in his early twenties, Gap sweater over Gap jeans and probably Gap fucking underwear, held his hands up. He squirmed in his seat like he wanted to go somewhere, but he didn't know how to get there.

"You honk that shit one more time and I'm gonna fucking end you."

I don't know if he heard a goddamn word through the window, but he saw the gun, the look on my face and he got my message. I went back to the car, took a deep breath, and said, "Meet me there in forty-five minutes."

81
CLYDE

I situated Madeline and the baby in the back seat of our car and headed for home. Just like me and the guys planned, my phone rang.

"Hello," I said. Then I made agreeable and noncommittal sounds. It was Brent on the other end, helping me with my excuse. When I hung up I looked at my wife. "I have to go to the shop. The cops and insurance guys need to talk to me."

She blew out a breath but nodded. "I can't wait for this to be over with. I want a guard dog for the house. A big one. And I think I want a Taser, too. I want to nuke any mo-fo that comes near me and little Jane here."

"Jane?"

Madeline said she liked the name Jane. It was simple and she was a Jane Austen fan, which I never actually knew, so she wanted Jane for the first name and I could pick the middle name. We had talked about names. All kinds of names. Natalie. Morgan. Jessica. Lula. Now all of a sudden its Jane. Fine. She was alive and beautiful and I was going to end this shit so I could hold her forever.

I pulled into the driveway, never so happy to see our house. I helped them in, set little Jane in the bassinet, kissed her, kissed Madeline, and headed back out to my car.

82
BRENT

I hung up from talking with Clyde, gave him the excuse he needed to be able to leave the house. Thanks to the pharmaceuticals in my system, I wasn't feeling much of anything, so Ernie drove. Betty sat beside him and Sean's wife sat in the back with me. The Virginia forest was a blur outside the window. I wondered if this was what LSD or mushrooms was like. We had the plan down pat. Go in, get set up, get Sean clear, and blow Skeeter away. I still wasn't clear on how that was going to not be considered murder. When I brought it up, Ernie just said, "Don't worry about it, kid."

We couldn't get close enough to Clyde's Rentals to park, so we parked at Hertz. My foot was completely unusable, so I slung an arm over Linda and an arm over Betty and hobbled to the back door. Ernie carried the duffel bag of whatever weapons he'd managed to collect. I hadn't bothered to tell anyone I couldn't use a gun. I hoped it wouldn't matter. I was counting on Ernie or someone else to take Skeeter out of the picture.

It was almost laughable that we unlocked the back door to get into the storeroom when the entire front of the building had been destroyed. The storeroom was hot and muggy. No air conditioning. Ernie set his bag down and unzipped it. "Check the front," he said. Betty knelt to help him while Linda and I hobbled that direction. Blood stains splattered the floor, dried and crusted. Any security detail was long gone. The building would have to be leveled. Someone had strung up police tape, which had come loose and whipped around in the wind. I leaned on what was left of the counter as Linda took a look around. "Quite a mess," she said. She looked a little pale and sickly, kept rubbing her side. Guess I'd forgotten she'd been shot, too. "Where are all the cops?"

"Small business. Small priority," I said. "They'll have the Hertz and Enterprise security guards watching things. They'll do a half-assed job. So much for Homeland Security." I tried not to think about the fact that it was Clyde and his fucked up way of making money that was responsible for all of this. That, and my mistake with the SUV.

Wooden barricades had been set up beyond the small lot. I wondered if Skeeter would just crash on through or get out and move them aside. Then I wondered if maybe he'd just come in the back like we did. I hopped back to the storeroom and saw that Betty was standing guard, peeping out the door.

Ernie handed me a gun. "Hold this," he said. "It's yours until this is over. Get your finger off the fucking trigger, imbecile. Don't put it there until you're ready to shoot. And take the safety off before you fire it."

Right. Whatever. Dick.

83
SEAN

Skeeter insisted on stopping at a gas station. We had to drive five miles out of the way to get there. He climbed out and told me to fill the tank. He kept one had on the butt of the gun in his waistband and lifted a finger into the air with the other while we stood beside the pump. I figured he must have been hallucinating. He stood close to me, and I could smell his stench even over the smell of the gas. After a minute a guy came out the door the shop and walked our way. Skeeter dropped some folded bills on the ground. "Yo, man, you dropped this," the guy said and bent over. When he came up again he had palmed the bills and handed Skeeter a small package.

Great. Just fucking great.

I finished with the gas and climbed back into the car. At least if the guy was stoned he couldn't notice how nervous I was. I didn't know what Ernie had planned. I could only hope he didn't want me as dead as we all wanted Skeeter.

84
SKEETER

How many fat people live in Virginia? Four out of every five fat people in the world must live in Richmond. I swear to fucking God. And the asshole driving the car was no different. Clean as a whistle but still the stench of moldy skin poured off of him.

I knew one thing only...I was going to end this today. Take my money and go. Okay, I guess that's two things I knew. Or three. I was thirsty and I hadn't gone in to get anything to drink. Fucking fat fuck had to be watched. Fucker.

The airport always bugged me. Always. I hated Clyde Fucking McDowd and his fucking rental lot. I hated no trees and sunlight popping off all those windshields all over the place. I hoped they got that cop's body. Stupid dumb-ass fucker.

Some asshole had put up barricades. I made the fat fucker get out and move them while I kept the gun pointed at his back. Cops were all gone, which was a good thing. Mood I was in I'd have capped anyone standing in front of me. Except Mr. Sloppy, who had my cash inside.

We got closer and parked. I'm not stupid. I knew they were watching for me, waiting for me, so I kept Fats in front of me while we walked toward the front. I'd done a good job of taking out the front end, if I do say so myself. It was nice to know that Clyde would be thinking about me for a long time to come.

85
ERNIE

I was airborne in 1971 in 'Nam. I'd fly in, patrol, leave. I had diabetes thanks to Agent Orange, COPD thanks to smoking, and erectile dysfunction, but that was likely just because I was married to Betty. 'Nam was like one of those Dickens novels. "It was the best of times, it was the worst of times." Every so often, the air would go still and a guy just knew all hell was gonna break loose. Times like that, I'd get that flutter in my gut, like that first downward drop on a roller coaster. It was a heart in my throat feeling and I had it now, waiting for that punk assed tweaker to get close enough for me to end.

"I don't like the look in your eye," Betty said.

"That's because you don't recognize it," I said, slamming a clip into my .45.

"You're right. I don't."

I handed her the weapon. "Use it on the tweaker," I said. "You see him, you shoot."

She shook her head like I was nuts. And maybe I was. But I couldn't wait until the next reunion trip to DC to tell the guys about this.

"Car's coming," Linda said.

"Right. I'm ready."

86
CLYDE

I parked at Hertz and ignored the security guard who waved at me. No time, fellas. I got a crazy guy to deal with. I was still in scrubs. Dirty, smelly, wrinkled scrubs. I looked like I'd pulled the clothes out of medical waste. My building was ruined. I could see it from a block away. Ruined. Everything ruined. I went to the back door, hoping Skeeter wasn't there yet, hoping everyone else was. There were no red suitcases filled with cash. I'm sure Skeeter suspected that. During his more lucid moments, he wasn't exactly stupid. Close, but not exactly. So where did that leave us? Shoot first, ask questions later?

I kept my head down, hunched my shoulders, and jogged the last three hundred feet. When I looked up again, the old woman was holding the back door open for me.

I ducked in. The old man pressed a gun into my hand while my eyes adjusted to the dimness of the storeroom.

"I'll tell you what I told your squirrely friend there," he said, nodding in Brent's direction. Brent rolled his eyes. "Keep your fucking finger off the trigger until you want to use it. And don't fucking point it at me."

I lowered it and let it hang next to my thigh.

"What's next?" I asked.

"McDowd, you here?" Skeeter

Ernie put his fingers to his lips, then did a peace sign in the air, pointed his two fingers at his own eyes, then at me, then made a fist in the air, like we were all Navy Seals or something.

"Whatever," I said. I opened the door to the small area behind the counter and took a minute to absorb the destruction. I hadn't been quite prepared. I thought it looked bad on the outside. "Here," I said.

Skeeter had Sean in front of him. It was like a toothpick hiding behind a building. There was no way I could hit Skeeter with any kind of bullet. Even if I fired through Sean at point blank range, that bullet would only make it halfway through the belly before it stopped. Sean Griffin, I decided, would make an excellent CSI dummy. I could picture those techs testing all sorts of bullets on that big mount of flab he carried in front of him.

"You got that suitcase?" Skeeter asked.

"In the back."

He peeked out from behind Sean's back. "The fuck it doing back there? Get it. Let's get this over with."

"Okay," I said. "Okay."

I hoped everyone was in place and knew their role.

87
BRENT

I spoke to Ernie. "I really think the women should be somewhere else in case this gets ugly." Lord knows everything else had, so it was a legitimate concern.

Linda spoke up first. "It's my goddamn husband out there." I waited for Betty to say something about it being her son-in-law, but she stayed quiet. We didn't have time to argue the point because Clyde came into the back room with a worried look on his face.

"He's got Griffin and he's using him like a shield."

Ernie looked thoughtfully at the door. "That's a lot of shield."

"I can't hit him," Clyde said. I knew I couldn't. Didn't feel like it even needed saying.

"I might could do," Ernie said, scratching the stubble on his chin.

"Daddy, don't you dare take a shot unless you know you can get him," Linda said. Since the first time I met her the Detroit was gone out of her voice and the full Virginia came back. The deeper we got into this both she and Ernie betrayed their backwoods lineage more and more.

Clyde was antsy. "I gotta get back out there." He was looking to Ernie for an answer like a soldier waiting for his commanding officer.

"Lemme think, lemme think," Ernie said.

I grabbed a banker's box of old receipts off the pile of strewn wreckage, kinda glad I'd procrastinated with the filing of last year's paperwork. "Give him this," I said. "Tell him it's the money. He lets Griffin go and we've got him."

I couldn't believe I was so eager to orchestrate another man's death, but I recognized it was the only way to tie up the last loose end of this thing. It was Skeeter's own damn fault, too. If he'd just faded away and recognized when the game was over this wouldn't be necessary.

"It might work," Ernie said.

I handed over the box to Clyde who took it and hefted the weight a moment. How he thought it compared to thirty grand or whatever amount Skeeter thought he was gonna get, I don't know. He took it through the door with him though, so it was a plan.

Me and Ernie crowded the doorway to peek through and watch the action, guns at the ready to bust in at the right moment and end this. I already knew, and I think Ernie did too, that I would let him go through the door first.

88
SEAN

Clyde came back with a box. I sure as hell wished I knew what they were up to because that box didn't have my Detroit money it, I was sure of that. Why move it from a suitcase to a cardboard box? But at least they had a plan. More than I had right then.

Clyde set the box on a part of the counter that wasn't crumbled in a heap.

"Here you go, Skeeter. Take it and get the hell out of here."

"Walk it on over here," the greasy little monkey said.

"You want it, you come get it."

Skeeter shuffled his feet a bit, moving nervously behind me. He shoved me forward. "You get it." He hid behind me like I was a tree or a big rock. I'd never been more committed in my life to dropping a few pounds.

I locked eyes with Clyde to see if there was anything I could get from just a look. Some clue, some sign of the best course of action. I got nothing so I stepped forward. My feet crunched over bits of the crash. Glass and parts of the chewed up counter where I'd pitched the fit that got me saddled with the wrong damn car. What a stupid mistake. I could have avoided all this if I'd only chosen to suffer through a few days of a stinky car. It might have been worth it or maybe Linda's never-ending nagging about it would have been a worse fate than getting shot and chased and the whole damn thing.

I moved slow, trying to get something out of Clyde. He watched behind me, keeping an eye on Skeeter. When he flicked his eyes to mine I tried to give him a lifted eyebrow, a tight lip, something to let him I know I wanted a cue. Do I duck and cover? Do I do what he says? Is that really my money in the box?

Setting my life right counted on giving that money back once I got home to Detroit. It may have been a pipe dream at that point, but the alternative wasn't pretty. And I'd seen a whole lot of not pretty the past few days.

Somewhere in the mix of odors—Skeeter's three-day sweat, the lingering sting of gasoline from the crash, the slightly foul smell of blood from the cop they said got shot here—I swore I got a whiff of Ernie's after shave. He was old school, my father-in-law. He had smelled the same for fifty years. I didn't even know the brand when I saw it in his bathroom at the house. Some old timey concoction he probably bought in bulk before the company went out of business. But it was distinct and it was there.

As soon as it settled in my nose, I knew it was going to be all right.

89
BRENT

I felt Ernie tense up next to me. The gap between Sean and Skeeter was growing and he saw a window for action. I hated to throw a wet blanket over the whole affair, but I felt it was a fair question worth asking so I whispered in his ear, "Are we really going to gun this man down in cold blood after we lured him here with a lie?"

The way I phrased it made it sound even worse than it was.

Ernie turned to me, gave me his best grizzled old veteran stare. This was another guy who liked the smell of napalm in the morning.

"That skinny tweaker son-of-a-bitch shot my daughter. Brought violence to my home. Tried to kill me and my wife. Not to mention he's a scumbag, drug dealing waste of space who wouldn't be worth the money it cost to jail him. If he turns and runs I'll shoot him in the fucking back and still sleep easy tonight."

Ernie turned away from me again, his argument made. Hard to contradict any of it. Still, it was killing a guy...

Ernie's boot on the door sounded as loud as a gunshot, or so I thought. He took two steps into the former lobby of Clyde McDowd Rents and fired off a shot. Now that was loud, especially compared to the shots when we were all outside.

Against my better judgment I was right on his heels.

Griffin did the right thing and hit the decks. The box of receipts dumped on top of him as he went down. Clyde was moving behind the broken counter and struggling to get the gun free from his belt. I had mine out in my hand, but my finger wasn't even on the trigger. Ernie seemed to have this well in hand.

Skeeter fired back with a wild shot that went somewhere over our heads. He sprinted to the left, hot footing it across the floor full of shrapnel. I don't think Ernie's shot got him. That or he didn't care.

90
SKEETER

    A fuckin' ambush. Y'know what, it's gettin' so you can't trust a goddamn soul in this world.

91
CLYDE

By the time I got my gun out Skeeter was zipping across the floor so fast it looked like he was water-skiing on a lake. I knew the first time I met the little creep it would be bad news. I almost mentioned to Corgan that I didn't trust him and didn't want to work with him, but somehow admitting that I had doubts about Corgan's hiring practices was also an admission that taking me on as the go-between was maybe a bad idea.

I knew now that it was, but there was no time for hindsight with Skeeter skipping away across my lobby.

Ernie fired another shot but missed him. Maybe the old man wasn't the marksman he used to be. I had my gun out and was ready to take a shot—something to blast away the frustration and pain of the past few days—but before I could, Skeeter's forward momentum stopped.

He ran for where the door used to be, but didn't expect the post to be there. A thick metal beam that probably should have been holding up the ceiling or something jutted out in his path and he smacked that thing face first while paying more attention to where Ernie's shots were coming from than to where he was going.

He disappeared to the mess on the floor. I couldn't see a thing from behind the half counter where I was.

"Did I get him?" Ernie called out.

"I don't think so," I said.

Griffin spoke in a panicked whine. "Can I stand up? Can I run?"

"Stay down," commanded Ernie and then the whole place fell into silence. The crunch of feet moving slowly over the broken shards of my business meant someone was moving out there, but I didn't know who. Only a few hours earlier I thought this bullshit was behind me, but there I was lying to my wife again about where I was, not sure where the next bullet was coming from.

"Anyone see him?" I asked.

I got back nothing.

After a few more moments of silence I started to wonder if Skeeter had knocked himself out on the beam or if he'd caved his head in so much he was dead.

I poked my head out and saw Ernie in a low crouch. He caught my eye and made some hand motions I couldn't translate. I gave him a "What?" look. He rolled his eyes at me mouthed the words in over-exaggerated mime. I'm. Going. Over. There.

I nodded and held out my gun in a two handed grip for him to see as my way of saying I was backing him up. I saw him turn and make the same hand motions to Brent on the other side, then movement caught my eye.

The sound came a moment later and I could see Skeeter up and scrambling for the door. He stayed low and zig-zagged across the floor. Ernie broke off from his pantomime with Brent and took two shots that missed the mark. I lifted my gun and sighted down on Skeeter, though he was moving fast and I didn't have enough confidence in my shot to pull the trigger.

He reached what used to be the front glass doors. There used to be the bell that told us any time a customer walked in. There used to be the hours of operation sign, the open and closed sliding sign and our membership affiliation stickers for the various rental guilds and AAA approval ratings. All gone now.

My finger moved onto the trigger as Skeeter stood up a little straighter, his body almost through the door. He slipped and skidded sideways. I didn't fire, but I didn't have to. Skeeter slid and slammed his body into the twisted metal of what used to be the door frame. A thin silver strip of door molding was torn and bent out to the side. He caught it, or maybe it caught him, in the neck. It drove in sharply and poked out the other side.

Skeeter hung from the protruding metal and dripped blood down the former door frame. He twitched a few times, his legs spasming and piss staining the insides of his pants. And then, he stopped moving.

The room was still for a while as we all took it in, watching from our different corners of the room. Ernie was the first to stand up. He hung his pistol down by his side and sounded dejected when he said, "Damn it. That was supposed to be me that ended him."

Griffin still sounded desperate and reluctant to get off the ground. "Is that it? Is he dead?"

"Yeah," I said. "That about wraps it up."

92
BRENT

More cops. The FBI guy again. And more questions. Always the goddamn questions. I answered as best I could, keeping an eye on Skeeter's body. They'd tossed a sheet over it and techs scrambled around taking photos. He was good and dead, but I still half expected him to come at us again.

It was a kidnapping by a psychopath, plain and simple. No one was to leave town until all the questions had been answered and the matter cleared up. Like any of us had anywhere to go. I looked over at Sean Griffin. He had an arm slung around his wife. She'd been crying and didn't seem to want to leave his side. I finished with my questions and was shoved into an ambulance. My foot had opened up and was bleeding again. It was getting hard to talk through the pain and at last, they let me go. I gave a wave to Clyde as the ambulance pulled out. Then I let my eyes close and gritted my teeth against the ache in my foot.

93
SEAN

We finished with the cops and, thanks to the order not to leave town, headed back to Ernie and Betty's house. It looked like we'd be staying with them for a while.

We didn't get a chance to talk until almost midnight, when Ernie sat us all down on the deck with beers and Betty passed around a tray of cheese and crackers.

"I think you should call your brother," Ernie said. "Return the money you took."

"And go to jail," I finished.

He shook his head. "You won't go to jail. He's an ass and he screwed you. Take whatever happens like a man and you can't go wrong."

God help me I was actually starting to like the guy.

His eyes narrowed and he looked hard at me and Linda. "The pair of you are a couple of fuck ups," he said.

"Daddy!"

Ernie just shrugged. "Your kids are rotten and the way you treat each other is rotten."

"Ernie," Betty said with a warning in her voice.

"You're pretty pathetic too, woman. So am I for that matter." He took a draw on his beer. "But we're family. And we need to stick together."

I didn't know what that meant, exactly, but I knew then that we would work it out, me and Linda and our kids and Ernie and Betty. Family. Maybe we'd stay in Virginia. Maybe I'd go to jail. I didn't know. Linda took my hand and gave it a squeeze. Whatever happened, I figured we really would be okay if we just stuck together.

94
CLYDE

I drove home in a haze from the car lot. Agent Stu Trumble had told me not to leave town. I apologized to him for the badge but he waved me off. "Just a name tag," he said. "The real one is in my pocket."

I parked the car and climbed out. I stood and stared at the house for a minute, wondering if I was still welcome inside, hoping Madeline could forgive me.

The living room was dark and cool when I stepped in. My girls were on the couch and little Jane was breastfeeding. It hit me like a fist in the gut. Perfection. My family. Who the fuck cared if we had to scrimp and save for college? Good stuff didn't come easy. And this was good stuff.

"Hi," I said.

Madeline's face was drawn and worried when she looked at me. "You look like hell."

"I've been a total dick."

"Yeah. But we have Jane. And we have each other. I think we'll be okay."

I moved to hug her, but she held up a hand. "You are not touching me or this baby until you shower and throw those clothes away." I smiled and headed for the bathroom. "And brush your teeth for the love of God."

Yeah. We'd be okay.

THANKS

We'd like to thank Eric Campbell and the good people at Down & Out Books for all their hard work. JT Lindroos for the excellent cover. Jake Hinkson, Anonymous-9 and Bill Craig for the kind words. And to our families for their continued love and support.

ABOUT THE AUTHORS

JB Kohl and Eric Beetner met online through a mutual love of classic crime fiction and film noir. Eric read Jennifer's debut novel, *The Deputy's Widow*, and loved it. When he sent her a story of his, a partnership was born. They have written four full novels together despite never having met in person.

Their first two collaborations, *One Too Many Blows To The Head* and the sequel, *Borrowed Trouble*, garnered praise from Megan Abbott, Rebecca Cantrell, Kelli Stanley and many more for their evocation of classic noir film and fiction in mood and style. *Over Their Heads* is a contemporary thriller which sees Kohl and Beetner at their most playful and exciting.

OTHER TITLES FROM DOWN AND OUT BOOKS

See www.DownAndOutBooks.com for complete list

By Anonymous-9
Bite Hard

By J.L. Abramo
Catching Water in a Net
Clutching at Straws
Counting to Infinity
Gravesend
Chasing Charlie Chan
Circling the Runway

By Trey R. Barker
2,000 Miles to Open Road
Road Gig: A Novella
Exit Blood
Death is Not Forever

By Richard Barre
The Innocents
Bearing Secrets
Christmas Stories
The Ghosts of Morning
Blackheart Highway
Burning Moon
Echo Bay
Lost

By Eric Beetner and JB Kohl
Over Their Heads (*)

By Eric Beetner and Frank Scalise
The Backlist (*)

By Rob Brunet
Stinking Rich

By Dana Cameron (editor)
Murder at the Beach: Bouchercon Anthology 2014

By Stacey Cochran
Eddie & Sunny

By Mark Coggins
No Hard Feelings (*)

By Tom Crowley
Vipers Tail
Murder in the Slaughterhouse

By Frank De Blase
Pine Box for a Pin-Up
Busted Valentines and Other Dark Delights
A Cougar's Kiss (*)

By Les Edgerton
The Genuine, Imitation, Plastic Kidnapping

By A.C. Frieden
Tranquility Denied
The Serpent's Game
The Pyongyang Option (*)

By Jack Getze
Big Numbers
Big Money
Big Mojo
Big Shoes (*)

By Keith Gilman
Bad Habits

(*)—Coming Soon

OTHER TITLES FROM DOWN AND OUT BOOKS

See www.DownAndOutBooks.com for complete list

By Richard Godwin
Wrong Crowd (*)

By William Hastings (editor)
Stray Dogs: Writing from the Other America

By Matt Hilton
No Going Back
Rules of Honor (*)
The Lawless Kind (*)

By Terry Holland
An Ice Cold Paradise
Chicago Shiver

By Darrel James,
Linda O. Johnston &
Tammy Kaehler (editors)
Last Exit to Murder

By David Housewright &
Renée Valois
The Devil and the Diva

By David Housewright
Finders Keepers
Full House

By Jon & Ruth Jordan (editors)
Murder and Mayhem in Muskego
Cooking with Crimespree

By Andrew McAleer & Paul D. Marks
(editors)
Coast to Coast (*)

By Bill Moody
Czechmate
The Man in Red Square
Solo Hand
The Death of a Tenor Man
The Sound of the Trumpet
Bird Lives!

By Gary Phillips
The Perpetrators
Scoundrels (Editor)
Treacherous

By Robert J. Randisi
Upon My Soul
Souls of the Dead
Envy the Dead (*)

By Ryan Sayles
The Subtle Art of Brutality (*)
Warpath (*)

By Anthony Neil Smith
Worm

By Liam Sweeny
Welcome Back, Jack (*)

By Lono Waiwaiole
Wiley's Lament
Wiley's Shuffle
Wiley's Refrain
Dark Paradise

By Vincent Zandri
Moonlight Weeps

(*)—Coming Soon

CPSIA information can be obtained
at www.ICGtesting.com
Printed in the USA
LVOW12s2349280717
543065LV00001B/204/P